Bumper Book of
Ghost Stories

BUMPER BOOK OF GHOST STORIES

Edited by Mary Danby

School Book Fairs

CONTENTS

KEPT IN
Rosemary Timperley

She looked up at the clock on the classroom wall. It was just past four. 'You will stay here for half an hour,' she said, in a voice icy with disapproval. 'I will then come and tell you that you may go.' And she marched out, closing the door behind her.

It's not fair, thought Tom. I wasn't playing up any more than the others were. It's just that I always seem to get picked on. That's the worst of having red hair. You stand out like a sore thumb. Same with fatties. Old Tub often gets picked on, just because he's big . . .

But today it had been Tom who'd born the brunt of Miss Lambert's wrath when the class grew disorderly. And, if he were honest, he couldn't blame Lanky – as they all called their skinny teacher – for being wrathful. The boys *did* torment her. They were all as bad as each other. They scorned her subject, of course: English. Fancy *teaching* English. I mean, it was daft, when they could all speak it already. As for *poetry*. Talk about waste of time.

Thus Tom sat brooding resentfully. Yet he didn't actually hate Lanky. She was quite pretty, really, and younger than the other female teachers on the staff. It was just that she was too inexperienced to keep order, and the temptation to fool about was too strong to resist.

Rain began to fall outside. The drops tapped the classroom panes with ghostly fingers. Like the spirit that raps on the window at the beginning of *Wuthering Heights*. Winter rain. Already it was dark. The room felt like a lighted prison in the middle of a black landscape, or wasteland. Well, he didn't *have* to stay. He could just walk out. But he hadn't quite the nerve to do that. It was one thing to defy a teacher when you had all the others to back you up, but when it was just you and her – better be careful. Don't want to get reported to the Head.

On the face of it, there was nothing frightening about being kept in for half an hour. It was just a bore. Yet of a sudden Tom did feel afraid in this classroom cage. A school is such a haunted place when everyone, or almost everyone, has gone home, shuffling in the bus queue, piling on to the bus, taunting the conductor. Yes, a haunted place now. Corridors echoing with silent footsteps of the past. Cloakrooms holding up their empty iron hooks, like beckoning fingers, or weird pieces of modern sculpture which people pretended to understand but no one did. The assembly hall vast and dark, like a deserted ballroom after a dance of death.

Tom began to shiver with apprehension. Suppose someone came to murder him! – slipped in by a side door, tiptoed up the stairs, approached the lighted room – walked in – now. There'd be no escape. Lanky Lambert would be in the staff room on the floor below. Even if she heard him scream, she wouldn't reach him in time. Anyway, she wouldn't care if he did get murdered. Probably be relieved.

He turned to gaze out of the window but could see nothing except his own white face, flare of red hair, and the bright room behind him. He pressed his face to the glass. Then he could see out. But there was nothing to see. Only the wet dark.

Then he almost froze with terror, for he heard the

door behind him softly open and close again, and then a funny little click. The murderer! With a gun?

I mustn't show I'm afraid, he told himself. I must be quite calm. I'll just turn round, slowly and casually – and see who is there.

He turned round, slowly, casually, putting on a proud expression. Then – Oh, the relief! It was only a boy. A younger boy than himself, too. A scared-looking, pale-faced boy. Must be a first-former, thought Tom, as the kid wasn't in regulation uniform. In theory, school uniform was compulsory; in practice, parents who were hard up were given time to provide the necessaries.

Tom didn't recognize the boy, but that wasn't surprising. One didn't take much notice of first form kids. It would be stupid to do so when you were in the third. But since there were only the two of them in the room, things were different. Tom was glad to see the other. He grinned and said, 'Hello, mate. You kept in too?'

'Aye,' answered the boy, a countrified burr in his voice.

'Who's got it in for you then?'

'Old Lanky,' said the kid.

'Same here. Been fooling around, have you?'

The youngster nodded.

'Well, don't look so scared,' said Tom. 'She won't eat us.'

'She'll come with the cane,' said the other.

'No. Not her. It's against the law, anyway. Only the Head's allowed to wallop you, and even that's on the way out.'

'She'll come with the cane,' the other repeated.

'If she does,' joked Tom, 'we'll tell her that we'll have the law on her, and if she takes no notice, it'll be two to one and we'll get the terrible weapon from

11

her.' He felt thoroughly cheered by the fact that the other boy was even more uneasy than he had been. That made Tom feel nicely superior.

'What's your name?' he asked now.

'Bill Farrow.'

'Mine's Tom Arden. What did you do to annoy Lanky?'

'Shot a dead spider at her with my catapult.'

Tom gave a hoot of laughter. 'That's great! We never do anything as off-beat as that. We just talk and mess around.'

Then he noticed something queer. The room seemed to be darkening and the air was becoming hard to breathe. There was an acrid smell. Smoke!

'There's a fire somewhere,' he said. 'The smoke's creeping in here. We'd best get out, Bill. I knew something bad was going to happen! I was feeling dead scared before you came,' he admitted now. 'Come on.' He made for the door.

'That's no use,' said Bill. 'She locked it.'

'Lanky? 'Course she didn't. Teachers don't have keys to the ordinary classrooms. Only for the labs.'

'She locked it,' Bill repeated.

'Don't be daft!' Confidently, Tom approached the door and turned the handle. The door didn't budge. He twisted the handle again, this way and that; shook the door. No use. Now he remembered that click he'd heard. She *had* locked it!

The corridor outside, which he could see through the glass top of the door, was dense with smoke. The smell of burning was growing stronger. Tom banged hard on the door. 'Help!' he cried.

'That's no good,' said Bill. 'No one will hear. She'll be over at the other building, fetching the cane. But she always makes you wait before she comes

12

and uses it. You feel it worse that way, when you have to wait. She knows that. She's hard.'

'Never mind about the cane,' said Tom. 'That's peanuts now. We're locked in here and the place is on fire. We've got to get out.' He ran to the window and opened it. The rain had stopped with apparent abruptness. The darkness outside was thick with smoke. As much of it seemed to be coming in through the window as being let out. And they were three floors up. It was too far to jump without breaking your legs or even killing yourself. Anyway, what would they jump *into*? A blindness of smoke . . .

He closed the window again. He was terrified inside himself but determined not to let the younger boy see that.

'I know what we'll do,' he said, with calm matter-of-factness. 'We'll break the glass at the top of the door, then climb over and out. At least we'll be better off in the corridor than in here. The fire might not be quite everywhere yet. There are several stair-cases for us to try, and the fire escape.'

He looked round for something hard with which to smash the glass. There was nothing. He took off his left shoe, aimed its heel at the glass, then drew his arm right back and gave the glass a terrific wallop with the shoe's heel. The glass cracked.

'Look, it's coming,' he said triumphantly. He banged again and again, harder and harder. The glass shattered and fell in slivers on both sides of the door. Smoke billowed chokingly into the room. Tom dragged on his shoe again then, coughing and splutt-ering, tied his handkerchief round his face to cover his mouth and nostrils. Then he turned to the younger boy.

'Got a hankie?' he asked.

'No.'

'Well, never mind. You'll just have to stick it out. This is what we'll do. We'll move this desk to the door – so! Now, women and children first – that means you, Bill. Climb on to it, over and out.'

But Bill was no longer listening. He'd flown into a complete panic. He was rushing up and down among the desks, flapping his arms, as if thus he could get rid of the clouds of smoke, beating on him like great grey wings. He was sobbing and choking, all self-control gone.

'Bill Stop that!' Tom cried, as loudly as he could through the muffling of the handkerchief. 'Come here at once, you silly idiot! Come and climb on this desk and then jump through the gap. Bill!' He lunged forward and tried to grab hold of the boy, but the other eluded him. Tom couldn't even touch him. It was almost as if he were afraid of Tom as much as of the smoke.

'All right! All right!' shouted Tom. 'I'll climb over and out, then stand on the other side and catch you, so you won't fall. Now for Pete's sake calm down!'

He mounted the desk, gripped the sides of the doorway where the glass was fragmented, felt slivers of the stuff cut his hands, felt blood begin to flow, ignored it, scrambled through, grazing his cheek, tearing the sleeve of his blazer – then jumped.

He was out.

Now he stood, still enveloped in smoke, half-blind and gasping with it.

'Come on, Bill! Climb up and jump through! I'll catch you!'

'I can't – I can't – ' Bill's voice was little more than a choking moan.

'You must!' yelled Tom. 'You must! Come *on*!' He was beginning to lose control himself now, out of fear and desperation. There were sobs in his voice.

His eyes were streaming, tears caused by both smoke and emotion.

He looked through the gap into the classroom, but he couldn't see anything properly any more, and he couldn't climb back to find Bill because he had nothing out here to stand on.

'If you stay in there, you'll burn to death!' he called gaspingly, trying to terrorise Bill into activity – although the kid was terrified already – and who wouldn't be?

This time there was no reply from within.

He's passed out, thought Tom.

'I'll get help!' he cried to the grey, stifling emptiness. But his voice seemed to be flung back at him, flung back dully from the blanket of smoke. His senses swam. He couldn't breathe. He tore the handkerchief away from his face, because it now seemed to be trapping more of the smoke than it was keeping at bay. And the last thing he saw before he fell unconscious to the floor was a hot redness of flame worming its way round the top of the nearest staircase . . .

When he came to, Lanky Lambert was bending over him. She looked concerned and compassionate, her thin little face all anxiety.

'Tom, why did you?' she said. 'What got into you?'

The corridor light was on. There was no smoke. No smell of burning. No red glow from the stairs. Rain was falling outside, tap-tap-tapping against the panes, sending messages in some secret code.

'Let me help you up. You're bleeding, child. Come along to the staff room. There's a First Aid box there.'

She began to half-support him along the corridor,

then his head cleared. 'Wait!' he said. 'Bill's still in there. He passed out before I did.'

'You've been dreaming. No one else is there.'

He insisted on going back to look.

They had some difficulty in getting the classroom door open, as the desk was pushed up against it, and they had to tread carefully to avoid the pieces of broken glass on the floor, but Lanky was right – the classroom was empty.

'Why did you do it?' Miss Lambert insisted, as she cleaned and bandaged his cuts in the staff room. 'Why break the glass and climb out instead of just walking out, if you really couldn't bear being kept in any longer?'

'You'd locked the door.'

'I certainly had not. You know that. You walked into the room to have a look a few minutes ago.'

'You must have unlocked it when I was unconscious.'

'No! It was not locked!'

'There was the fire,' said Tom.

'There's no fire.'

'All that smoke. Where did it go?'

'There never was any smoke. I came up when I heard the glass breaking and you shouting. I wondered what on earth was happening. When I reached you, you were just coming round from a faint. You've had some sort of hallucination.'

'There was a fire, and Bill Farrow was with me. He said you'd kept him in too and you were coming with a cane.'

'Me? I've never used a cane in my life and never would, however naughty you all are. Also there's no pupil in the school called Bill Farrow. None of it happened, Tom.'

She neatened up the last of the little bandages.

'There we are. Now you're almost as good as new. The cuts aren't so very bad. You were lucky. When I think what could have happened – ' She shivered. 'Now I'm going to see you safely home. But first I'll slip down to the caretaker's den and ask him to clear up the glass before the children arrive tomorrow. We don't want people cutting themselves. Wait for me here.'

She left the room. Tom leaned back wearily in the comfortable chair. Talk about 'bewitched, bothered and bewildered'. He didn't know whether he was coming or going. And he simply couldn't understand what had happened!

In ten minutes or so, Lanky was back. 'Ready, Tom? I'll drive you home.'

They left the school building together, in the rain. No fire anywhere. No smoke. The school in darkness now except for a light burning in the caretaker's room. Lanky's little red mini-car awaited them in the car park. They climbed in.

'How are you feeling now?' she asked.

'Peculiar, but otherwise all right.'

'Peculiar indeed!' she echoed him.

When they reached his home, she explained to his parents what had happened.

'You broke the glass?' said his father incredulously.

'I had to, Dad. There was this fire. I *thought* there was a fire. And there *was*! Believe me!'

His father looked at Lanky, who nodded. 'I do believe him. Mr Arden. He's had some weird sort of experience in there. My guess is that he dozed off out of boredom, then had a kind of dream-awake. I suggest you keep him at home tomorrow and take him to the doctor. His cuts are nothing – I disinfected them very carefully – but he's had a mental upset.'

'I'm not mentally upset,' protested Tom. 'Seeing

17

that it all happened – or seemed to happen,' he admitted, 'I behaved very sensibly. I had to get out. And it wasn't my fault that I couldn't get Bill Farrow out too. He wouldn't come. Or couldn't.'

'There is no Bill Farrow, child,' sighed Lanky, and then took her leave.

Tom's mother put him to bed, fussing over him, like an old hen, behaving as if he were little again. Exhausted by the ordeals of the afternoon and evening, he slept.

In the morning he came down to breakfast, feeling fit as a fiddle.

'I shan't stay at home to be mollycoddled,' he announced. 'I'm not going to see any old doctor. I'm going to school. I'm *all right*, Mum, honest. And there's sure to be a row over that broken glass, so the sooner I get that over with, the better. It's worse if you have to wait – ' He shivered slightly, recalling Bill's words about waiting. What *had* happened to Bill?

'There won't be a row over the glass,' said his mother. 'Miss Lambert is going to speak to the Head this morning and explain. She rang us up last night, after you were asleep in bed. We thought we'd wait till morning to tell you what she said.'

'What did she say?'

'When she got home to the flat she shares with a history teacher, she told her flat-mate about your strange experience. Apparently this other teacher has made a special study of the history of schools in this area, and at your school, about fifty years ago, there was a fire. A boy who'd been locked in one of the classrooms was burned to death. Apparently he'd been kept in by the then head teacher, a woman called Miss Lancaster.'

'Lancaster? I wonder if they called her "Lanky",' Tom murmured.

'It's a sad story,' his mother continued, 'but Miss Lambert thought you should know about it, and her friend would like to talk it over with you one day. In fact, you've been invited there to tea. She says you must be psychic – '

'Never mind about psychic,' Tom interrupted, 'I'm in trouble enough already, and if I don't put my skates on I'm going to be late!'

He swallowed the last of his breakfast coffee and shot out of the house. He puzzled over it all, of course, as he ran through the streets, becoming abnormally out of breath – and no wonder, after all that smoke he'd inhaled – except that there hadn't been any smoke – except that there had – hadn't – had – Might be interesting to have a talk with that friend of Miss Lambert's . . .

As he tore into the school, only just on time, the caretaker came out of his den and called: 'Hey! Tom! Tom Arden!'

'What is it?' Tom gasped. 'Don't hold me up!'

'You was the one broke the glass?'

'Yes.'

'Well, boy, I found this when I was clearing up. Is it yours?'

He passed a handkerchief to Tom, who took it. Then the man laughed a little. 'You kiddies,' he said, shaking his head. 'How do you manage to get your things into such a dirty mess?'

For that handkerchief *was* in a dirty mess. It was dark grey with soot – and it stank of smoke.

MACKRIN MAINS
Kay Leith

'There isn't even a hint of another house. There's just nothing for miles and miles but hills and trees and heather. There are trout streams and marshy places. The house is two-storied – combe-ceilings upstairs – and although the stonework is all right, the woodwork is terrible and there are lots of slates missing from the roof.'

Sylvia wondered if her mother was pitching it too strong, and bit back the words that threatened to spill out and spoil everything. They had agreed to paint the picture as it really was: no romantic frills, and no displays of gleeful enthusiasm.

That Sunday expedition, whilst her father had finished off his latest canvas in preparation for his summer exhibition, had borne fruit. The search had taken months. They had seen so many houses which were either out of their price range, or were too near to other houses and therefore did not come within their terms of reference. It was not that they intended to abandon civilization – they merely wanted a little less of it.

'What's the decorative condition?' asked Colin.

'Decorative condition!' snorted Maggie. 'What wallpaper there was has fallen off because of the damp. I'm not sure about the colour of the last coat of paint, because it's discoloured where it hasn't actually peeled away. I assure you, apart from the stonework, it's a mess.'

Sylvia's heart sank. Her mother had gone too far and killed the whole idea. But her father, strangely enough, appeared to be more interested just because they weren't trying to blind him with its advantages.

'You say there aren't any other houses for miles . . .' he mused.

'Oh, yes,' said Maggie grudgingly, darting a sly twinkle at Sylvia. 'It has that in its favour. It's isolated, all right. No doubt about that. But nobody could live there until the roof has been repaired.'

'The joists – what about the joists?'

'From what I could see through the trapdoor, which wasn't much, they seem all right.'

Colin flung down his paint brush and got up from the easel. He stared, first at Maggie, then at Sylvia, and shook his head in puzzlement. 'I can't understand it. It sounds just what we've been looking for, so why aren't the pair of you all agog and singing its praises?'

Sylvia shot a glance at her mother, apologetically, traitorously. 'I like it, Dad.'

Colin sat down again. 'Well, that's something, at any rate.'

'And I like it, too,' admitted Maggie, grinning.

'Well?'

His wife spread deprecating hands. 'It's just that we don't want to pressure you into agreeing to take the house. There's so much that requires to be done to make it habitable, and we just don't have the money to pay somebody to do it for us. It would mean a great deal of hard work.'

'What about water and electricity?'

'There's a well with a pump, but no electricity.'

'Hmmm. . . .'

Maggie sighed. 'Perhaps we ought to forget about it?'

21

Just then the thunderous roar of the motorbike belonging to the boy downstairs drowned out all thought. This was followed by the crash of a door, the thud of feet on the stairs, and the shouts of children.

Maggie's and Colin's eyes met, and an unspoken decision was arrived at. Sylvia gave a quiet smile. Their ability to read each other's minds was sometimes uncanny.

Sylvia remembered the first time she had noticed it. They had gone to the zoo. It was very hot, and they paused to rest at a bench. Without speaking, her father rose and walked off. Sylvia looked up at her mother questioningly, but the latter did not seem concerned.

'Where has Dad gone?'

Her mother smiled, slightly astonished. 'Didn't you hear him say that he was going to buy some ice cream?'

'But dad didn't say anything – '

'Oh yes, he did. I distinctly heard him.'

It became a family joke – a game. Sylvia found it quite easy when she concentrated. The three of them were so close that they were unable to decide whether they really had telepathic powers, or whether, because they knew each other so well, divining each other's thoughts and wishes was a natural ability, and was available to anyone willing to work at it.

They left Glasgow before dawn next day and gained their first glimpse of the purple ridges of the Monadhliath mountains at about eleven o'clock.

'There's a small signpost on the right when we go over a hump-back bridge,' said Sylvia. 'It says "To Lochan Luoghair", or something like that.'

'Yes,' agreed her mother. 'And we turn right there and carry on till we come to an old tree.'

'Shall we stop and drink our coffee now? I'm parched.'

'Oh, no, Colin. We're so near now. Let's wait till we get there.'

On each side of the narrow road were fields with barren, rock-strewn earth and clumps of rowan and birch. There was the occasional stone-built cottage, and once they passed the high walls and wrought-iron gates of what must have been a large mansion, but all they could see of it was one crenellated turret above the surrounding trees.

'Look,' said Colin. 'It has a light at the gate, which means that there is electricity up to this point at any rate. Is it much farther?'

'Only another four or five miles – not far,' said Maggie excitedly. 'Here's the bridge.'

'And there's the little signpost. Turn right here, Dad!' Sylvia wound down her window and breathed in the clean, sharp air. The last week in March, it was still chilly in the early morning and late evening, but during the day when the sun had had a chance to warm the air, it was pleasant. There was still snow on the peaks of the distant mountains, however.

To the left now was a heather-covered hill, to the right a small pine wood. Beyond a gnarled old alder a track led off – an overgrown track which must, in rainy weather, have been a treacherous river of mud.

The car bumped and lurched slowly up the track for what seemed miles, but was, in fact, quite a short distance, before the broken down, dry stone-walling of the garden of the house became visible.

The house itself stood high, as though the builder had specially chosen the site for its eminence. On closer inspection, however, it seemed to have been constructed on a circular platform of stones. The garden dropped away from the front door in a series of steps.

The wooden gate sagged drunkenly, finally collapsing altogether when Colin tried to push it open to make way for the car.

Finally, there they were, inside in the musty silence of the gloomy house. There was a large front room to the right, on the left a smaller room, and the passage led directly to the large kitchen at the back, with its huge iron range. The air was more damply cold there, seeming to strike through clothing and flesh to chill even one's bones.

Colin, coffee cup in hand, walked from room to room examining the flooring; then he made his way upstairs to check the first floor and the roof.

Sylvia found some dry wood and piled it in the kitchen fireplace, but the flames flickered only fitfully, then snuffed out, as though they found the grate too cold. She felt a curious, lonely dread, and went in search of her mother, who, after much frustrated pumping, was eventually rewarded by a gush of clear, cool water from the pump outside the kitchen door.

'I suppose it would have to be boiled until your father managed to check the drainage,' she said, turning to Sylvia. 'Well, darling, do you still like it?'

The girl grinned and nodded. 'Oh, yes, Mum.'

'You would have to stay with Gran in Glasgow during term-time.'

That thought had already occurred to Sylvia. There didn't seem to be any way round the problem – unless a suitable school could be found for her in the neighbourhood. The only one they had passed was miles away and had only two classrooms!

'May I have the little room on the left at the top of the stairs?' she begged.

Maggie laughed. 'We don't know yet whether your father will share our enthusiasm for the place, but if he does, the room's yours.'

There was a fearsome rumbling, as though the whole place were falling to pieces, and a slate crashed into the front garden.

'That's not a very good sign,' gasped Maggie, dashing upstairs, followed closely by Sylvia, to find her husband jumping from the trap door on the landing. 'Colin, are you all right?'

'Yes, yes. Don't fuss!' He dusted himself off and straightened up.

'Well?' demanded Maggie.

'The place has distinct possibilities. I'll go in to Inverness now and put down a deposit.'

Maggie clapped her hands with relief. 'Oh, I'm so glad!'

'Whee-oo!' yipped Sylvia, jumping up and down and making the floor boards rattle. 'Oh, how exciting! Please hurry, Dad, before somebody else decides to buy it.'

Husband and wife burst out laughing. 'I think it's been empty too long for much danger of that,' reasoned Colin.

'We'd better come with you, darling,' said Maggie. 'It will save your having to come back here.'

'Oh, Mum, let's stay a bit longer. There's so much to see,' begged Sylvia.

'Oh, all right,' agreed Maggie.

'I'll come back for you after I've seen the agent,' said Colin. 'I'll bring some food with me and we can picnic here.'

As the car drove off, bumping and lurching, mother and daughter went off to explore the mouldering farm buildings. There was an air of eternity about everything, something which willed that no matter how many changes were made by man, there would always be a reversion, a return to an ageless mossiness.

Later, they stood in the weed-infested front garden and looked at the house – the dirty paintwork, the washed-out, once white-rendered stones of the walls. A previous owner had planted sweet peas, which had seeded themselves time and again over the years and had eventually returned to their original pale purple. A stunted lilac tree would obviously not flower that year, and sickly green lichen threatened to choke the few live twigs of a raspberry bush.

'We'll root out all these weeds and put some fertilizer in the soil. The house will look crisp and clean when . . .' Maggie's voice trailed away and she passed a hand over her forehead, as though she had forgotten what she was going to say. She frowned and looked round, as though she had heard something.

A little worm of fear wriggled in Sylvia's mind, and the sky seemed to cloud over as the air grew still and bitingly cold. Bewildered, she saw her mother sway, as though pulled this way and that by unseen hands, and when she looked at the house she saw that the whitewash was gleaming and the clean windows had curtains on them. The roof was whole, and above it the sky sat leaden, like a predatory beast.

The red-painted door stood invitingly open, the iron shoe-scrapers shining with blacking. Her mother, strangely dressed in crude homespun, was walking slowly to the door.

Unable to resist, Sylvia followed like a sleepwalker. There was an enormous turmoil in her head. It was quite impossible to think. There was the well-scrubbed front step, outlined in white; there was the stone-flagged hallway with the rush matting. It was so important to go inside and find out. . . . Inside to the kitchen.

'Sylvia! Don't go!' The words came from inside her mind. She stopped, unwillingly. She wondered if her mother had heard, too.

'Mmmm . . .' she moaned. She tried harder. 'Mummy!' she burst out. 'Come back.'

She tried to force her legs to go to her mother. She looked down and saw that they were plaid-covered and that she was wearing moccasin-type shoes and thick, knitted stockings.

'I'm coming, Sylvia,' said something in her mind.

She made one stumbling step towards Maggie, feeling the strange heavy skirt flapping about her knees. It was like trying to walk in water; she seemed to be making no progress at all. With all her might, she took another step.

And all the while something from the kitchen exerted its incessant, unyielding attraction, as though pulling her towards what had to be done.

Suddenly, frantic and shouting, her father flung himself through the gate, heading for the doorway.

'Sylvia!' he yelled, diving into the hallway and dragging out his bemused wife. 'Get into the car, at once!'

Sylvia jerked out of her trance. At the gate she stopped in her headlong dash and looked back at the dirty windows and broken slates. Her legs were once again clad in jeans, her feet in shoes, and the sky was blue and clear.

'What happened, Colin?' asked the dazed Maggie as he helped her into the car. 'I don't understand. Why did I have to go into the house?'

'I don't know. Let's just get away from here – right now.'

'What made you turn back?'

27

Colin slipped the key into the ignition. 'It was Sylvia. I seemed to hear her cry out, and I felt you both must be in great danger. When I came, Maggie, you were in the hallway.' He stared at his wife's sensible jacket and slacks. 'And you were wearing a rough plaid dress. . . .'

'With a large brooch,' added Sylvia, shuddering uncontrollably. 'An old-fashioned, silver brooch with a yellow stone. Oh, please, Dad, let's go away from this place.'

Colin put the car in gear. 'The two of you must have been caught up in some episode from the past – some tragedy or other. I don't know. But we can't let that happen again. We'll just have to forget the whole business. There's something very peculiar and wrong about that place.'

They stopped at the first garage to refuel.

'So, you've been having a look at Mackrin Mains,' said the proprietor, unclipping the petrol hose.

'Mackrin Mains?' queried Colin hollowly.

'Yes. Mackrin was the man who built the place – way back in the beginning of the last century,' replied the man. 'Been renovated several times, but people don't seem to stay there long. Understandable, I suppose.'

'Why understandable?'

'Well, because of its history. Some places seem to attract evil – or maybe it's just that they can't rid themselves of the evil that's been perpetrated in them. I don't know. Anyway, it's been empty, off and on, since I was a lad.'

'What happened there?' asked Colin, hiding his impatience as, round-eyed and pale, Maggie and Sylvia listened from inside the car.

'Oh, it was too long ago for anybody around here to remember many of the details, but Mackrin was a pig-headed individual, so the tale goes. It was on that spot, he decided, and no other that he would build his farm house. The word 'mains', by the way, means a farm house.'

'Yes,' prompted Colin.

'Aye, well, build it he did, and he and his wife and child never knew a happy minute in it. Nobody knows what eventually happened to them. It was said the old ones took them.'

'The old ones?'

'Aye, the spirits belonging to the ring cairn,' explained the man. 'You see, Mackrin built his house on top of a ring cairn. He was told he'd offend the old ones, but as I said, he was a pig-headed man. He even had the effrontery to use the boar stone – that's a carved stone – as part of his kitchen wall.'

Sylvia now realised the significance of her dread of the kitchen. Could it have been an old sacrificial place? Her blood chilled, not for the first time that day.

'It's said,' continued the garage proprietor, well-satisfied with such an attentive audience, 'that the old ones won't be happy until the house has mouldered away completely and there is no stone of it left standing – except the boar stone, of course. Oh, it's been inhabited, but never for long. The old ones make sure of that.'

Silently, Maggie and Sylvia watched Colin get back into the car. As though in afterthought, he shouted a question to the garage proprietor. 'Can you remember the Mackrins' first names?'

The man was surprised. He scratched his head. 'Can't say I ever knew the names of the wife and lassie, but Mackrin himself was baptised Colin. Come to think of it, the tale goes that they disappeared off the face of this earth some time in March

29

over a century ago – the spring equinox, 'tis said.'
He laughed and nodded. 'Aye, and today's March
21st – just as near as you can get to it.'

The man waved them off, watching as the car
picked up speed on reaching the main road. 'Now,
why would they want to know the names of the
Mackrins?' he wondered.

'Dad, what is a ring cairn?' queried Sylvia.

'Oh, these ring cairns were built around the first
or second millenium, before even the Romans came.
Some say they had connections with the druids and
were places of sacrifice – human sacrifice.'

There was silence for some time as the trio came
to terms with what had happened. Fright gave way
to relief at their escape, and life suddenly became
very precious. The sunlight was brighter, the air
clearer, and their senses keener with the knowledge
that it had so nearly been taken from them.

Sylvia, remembering the rough feel of the long
skirt and the clumsy, thong-bound moccasins, ran a
grateful hand down her trousered legs. Trembling,
she reached out and touched the material of her
mother's jacket. Just to make sure, she leaned forward to check it wasn't homespun, dark green plaid,
held together at the neck with a heavy yellow-stoned
brooch.

Sensing the reason for her daughter's gesture,
Maggie caught her hand and shuddered in remem-
brance. 'If Sylvia had gone into the house . . . on
such a day as this . . . a sacrificial day . . .'

'But she didn't! The chain of events was broken
when I sensed her fear and she tried to get to you to
stop you,' said Colin Mackrin hoarsely. He was silent
for some minutes. 'If other people couldn't find happiness in that house, what chance would we have
had, with a name like Mackrin?'

THE HOUSE GHOSTS
Mary Danby

The street was grey with December rain as the post-man stopped outside Number 19 and took from the bundle of letters in his hand a pale mauve envelope addressed to Mrs Wetherby. He glanced about him, then furtively held it to his nose for a moment before slipping it through the letterbox. His face, as he turned away, showed clearly that he, for one, was happy not to be on the receiving end of a violet-scented letter.

In the hall of Number 19, Mrs Wetherby picked up the letter – a little gingerly, on account of the smell – and began to read it. Her eyes widened with dismay. 'Oh, no!' she groaned. 'How simply ghastly!'

Her daughter Wendy, on her way through to the kitchen, paused. 'What's up?'

'It's from Aunt Prudence,' said Mrs Wetherby. 'Your grandmother's cousin, remember? She came for a weekend once and you said you hoped she'd never come again. Well . . .'

'Yes . . . ?' said Wendy suspiciously.

'Aunt Prudence usually goes to Bournemouth for Christmas, to stay with her sister Mildred. *She's* pretty dreadful, too – all luncheon meat and dog hairs. We used to call her Aunt Mouldy. Anyway, it seems Aunt Prudence needs a break from her. "There's a train arriving around four o'clock on December 23rd," she says, "and no doubt I can find a taxi to bring me from the station. How nice that we shall all be together for Christmas." '

Wendy stood quite still, drinking in the horror of it all. Then she said: 'Must we? I mean, do we really have to? Couldn't you write back and say we've all got chicken-pox?'

'It's a bit late for that,' Mrs Wetherby said miserably. 'She's arriving the day after tomorrow.'

'But it's Christmas,' Wendy complained. 'We *can't* have her here for Christmas. She'll ruin everything. You know how putrid she is. She's a monster. Five-star.'

Aunt Prudence was one of those people who arrived and took over. Everything had to be organized her way – which was usually nobody else's way, and anyone daring to voice an opinion she didn't agree with was dealt a withering look and punished in some subtly infuriating way such as being sent to turn the house upside-down for Aunt Prudence's reading glasses, when all the time they were right next to her, in her handbag. ('Well, fancy that, now!') If the gas fire was on, Aunt Prudence chose the heat setting. When the daily newspaper arrived, Aunt Prudence would collar it – and read it maddeningly slowly. At mealtimes, she always took the first of everything, and the last. She was indeed monstrous.

'I suppose we'll have to buy her some sort of Christmas present,' said Mrs Wetherby, sighing heavily.

'A boa constrictor?' suggested Wendy.

The news of Aunt Prudence's visit filled the house with gloom. The lights on the Christmas tree seemed to dim to half their brightness, and the decorations sagged mournfully. Mr Wetherby sat for a long while, staring into space, while the two boys, Peter and Danny, wandered aimlessly from room to room, egging each other on in their disgust at the situation.

'Think of her voice,' said Danny. 'It's like a rusty chain saw.'

'She's a pig. Prudence Pig. Fat, greedy and revoltingly pink,' said Peter.

'Yuk!' said Danny. 'And she smells like carnations. Dead ones.'

'She goes on and on. On and on and on, she goes. On and on.'

'She always bags the best chair.'

'The biggest cake.'

'The crispiest potato.'

'I wish she'd go to Timbuctoo,' said Peter.

'Blinkistan,' said Danny.

'Where's that?' said Peter.

'Nowhere. I made it up.'

By the evening, however, they had more or less resigned themselves to the Coming of Aunt Prudence. 'We'll pretend she's not there.' But this was something of an optimistic idea, and it was a far from cheerful family which finally went upstairs to bed.

Later on, when the only remaining light came from the street-lamps outside, two shadowy figures gradually appeared in the armchairs on either side of the hearth. One was an elderly gentleman in a velvet smoking jacket, the other, a short, stoutish woman who wore a straight, ankle-length skirt topped by a lacy blouse, a long, jet necklace and a rather attractive maroon shawl she had crocheted herself. Albert and Victoria were brother and sister. About fifty years before the Wetherby family had bought Number 19, Albert and Victoria had lived there. Died there, in fact. And now they returned to it from time to time, as they had quite a fondness for the old grey building.

'House Ghosts,' they were known as, in the Order of Beyond.

Number 19 was strong and solid, made to last, with tall sash windows on either side of the glazed porch. In the days when Albert and Victoria lived there, a maid had scrubbed the steps once a week. Now the steps were dark and dingy, but the house was bright within, and the brother and sister were glad to hear it ring with laughter and the shouts of children.

'Such a shame,' said Victoria, tidying a strand of her silver hair into the bun at the nape of her neck. 'They always have such a jolly Christmas, and now that appalling Aunt Prudence is going to spoil it all. I remember when she came here before. She ate all the chocolate biscuits at tea.'

'Reminds me of Great Aunt Isobel,' said Albert. 'Now, she was almost worse, wasn't she. Never used to allow any fun at all. She said the noise of merrymaking was like the bells of Hell calling us to damnation.' He shuddered. 'I can see her now. Like a pencil, she was – tall and straight and grey.' His moustache quivered at the memory.

'The thing is,' said Victoria, 'what are we going to do about the dreaded Aunt Prudence?'

'Do?' queried Albert. 'I don't see what we *can* do. If she's coming, she's coming.'

Victoria gave a hopeful little smile. 'But, couldn't we . . . couldn't we make things just a bit . . . how can I put it . . . . *disturbing* for her?'

'Are you saying what I think you're saying?' Albert asked, frowning.

'Just this once . . . ?'

Albert shook his head. 'Out of the question, my dear. You know it's against the rules. We're allowed to visit, but we mustn't haunt. Otherwise we might be exorcised, and we wouldn't want that to happen. Remember Percy Blick.'

Percy Blick had been a friend of theirs, a one-time Town Councillor, now a Dear Departed, who had taken to floating wispily through the middle of council meetings and blowing cold air at the back of the mayor's neck every time he didn't like what was being discussed. Eventually, a priest had been called to get rid of him. Some words were said in Latin, and the priest sprinkled holy water here and there, and the next thing Albert and Victoria heard was that Percy had his Visitor's Pass taken away and had been banished to the Great Void for a year and a day.

'Remember Percy Blick,' Albert repeated. 'We wouldn't want that to happen to us. No – spectral appearances, moans, rattling chains . . . I'm afraid we couldn't risk it.'

Victoria thought for a while. 'Suppose we didn't actually *appear*,' she said slowly. 'Suppose there just happened to be one or two little accidents . . . Nothing that would make them suspect us, of course. But Aunt Prudence might find her stay the teeniest bit uncomfortable, don't you think?' She looked hopefully at her brother, who was sucking gently at his teeth as he considered the matter. 'I mean, we can't just sit here and do nothing at all,' she concluded.

'Hm . . . hm . . . Very well, then,' Albert said eventually, 'as it is in such a good cause. But we must take care not to let them think they are being haunted. Of course,' he added, 'I wouldn't even consider it, but for the memory of Christmas 1883, ruined so disastrously by the cheerless presence of Great Aunt Isobel. No, Aunt Prudence must be seen to.'

'Oh – spiffing!' said Victoria.

On the day before Christmas Eve, at about four-thirty in the afternoon, Aunt Prudence arrived. She wore a huge pink mohair coat, which made her look even more bulky than ever, and perched on her lilac-rinsed curls was a red pillbox hat, so that she could have been mistaken, at a distance, for a pink blancmange with a cherry on the top.

'Aunt Prudence. How nice,' said Mrs Wetherby, opening the door wide so that the pink blancmange could wobble into the hall. 'Children!' she called. 'Aunt Prudence is here. Come down and say hello.' There was no sound. 'At once!' she demanded.

Wendy appeared at the top of the stairs, and at that moment there was a violent crash as the front door apparently slammed itself shut. The noise was so loud that Aunt Prudence jumped sideways, and her little red hat slid down to her nose just as a paper-chain came unstuck from the ceiling and descended over her shoulders.

'Must have been the wind,' said a surprised-looking Mrs Wetherby.

'Hello, Aunt Prudence,' said Wendy, smothering a smile as she walked down the stairs. 'How Christmassy you look.'

'Don't smirk, girl. It doesn't become you,' said Aunt Prudence, readjusting her hat and removing the paperchain. 'Yes, you're too thin, I remember that. It's ugly to be so thin. Is tea ready, Helen? I'm famished.'

Mrs Wetherby led the way into the sitting-room and brought in a tray of tea and cakes. Danny and Peter at last came down to say a reluctant hello.

'One cake each,' said their mother.

As the two boys reached towards the plate, Aunt Prudence said smugly: 'Visitors first,' and stretched out a hand for the biggest and best – a large slice of chocolate cream gateau. But as she lifted it towards the gaping cavern of her mouth it somehow managed to slip out of her hand and land in a squidgy mess on her lap.

'What a horrible, clumsy little boy,' Aunt Prudence said to Peter, waving a pink, piggy finger at him. 'You jogged my elbow.'

Peter shook his head and looked toward his mother. 'I didn't. Honestly, I didn't. I wasn't even anywhere near.'

Aunt Prudence turned to Danny. 'Fetch a damp cloth,' she demanded. 'Damp, mind, not wet. And while you're doing that, I'll have the cake that would have been Peter's. Perhaps it will teach him not to answer back, eh?' She stretched her rosebud mouth into a smug smile. 'This one, I think . . .' Mrs Wetherby protested, but Aunt Prudence pretended not to hear. 'I do like a nice éclair,' she said. 'What a shame there's only the one.'

Later, when Mr Wetherby came home, the whole family settled down to watch the television. Aunt Prudence had brought her knitting – a large, shapeless splodge of turquoise and apricot, which, she said, was on its way to becoming a bedjacket. While she knitted, the balls of wool would keep slipping from her lap to the floor. No matter how securely she lodged them, they managed to roll off, and she tut-tutted to herself and made one of the children pick them up again. By the eighth time, she was getting very rattled indeed, but Danny and Peter were enjoying it all hugely, holding out their hands to catch the wool before it reached the floor.

Just then, the clock in the hall struck seven.

'Oh good, time for my programme,' announced Aunt Prudence.

Mr and Mrs Wetherby looked at each other.

'But we're watching this film,' said Wendy. 'There's still half an hour to go.'

'I always watch my programme,' Aunt Prudence persisted. 'Kindly switch over to the other channel.'

Wendy turned to her father for help, but he just shrugged his shoulders, as if to say: 'What's the use of fighting it? We might as well grit our teeth and suffer in silence.'

Aunt Prudence's programme turned out to be *The Oldies* – a long-running serial about life in an old people's home, which made her chortle and cluck and shake her head from side to side, while the Wetherby family sat about in various attitudes of boredom, wishing they could turn back to *Duel in the Dust*. After *The Oldies* had been on for two or three minutes, however, the picture began to go round and round.

'Really!' said Aunt Prudence, pursing her lips. 'Oh, do fix it, someone.'

Mr Wetherby fixed it. Then the colour faded to black and white. Mr Wetherby fixed it. Then the screen became covered with little white spots. Then zig-zag lines appeared. Then the sound went alternately loud and soft.

'I don't think much of this television,' complained Aunt Prudence. 'The one I have at home is a great deal better.'

'Well, go back to it, then,' muttered Danny under his breath.

'Let's try the other channel,' Wendy suggested hopefully. She pressed a button and, within seconds, all the faults vanished. 'Looks as though we'd better watch the film after all,' she said brightly.

'Hm,' grunted Aunt Prudence. 'It's never like this at Mildred's in Bournemouth. I dare say it's your Christmas tree lights. They use up all the electricity.'

When everyone was in bed that night, and sound asleep, Albert and Victoria once more took shape before the cold hearth. In their day, it would have been the dying embers of a good coal fire in front of them – and a thick, smoky fog outside. But Albert and Victoria didn't mind the absence of a fire; heat and cold had meant nothing to them for fifty years.

'Oh, isn't this good fun,' Victoria said gaily. 'Aunt Prudence is quite, quite dreadful, but I thought when you made her drop that cake I'd die laughing. Well, if I wasn't dead already, of course.'

Albert chuckled. 'What flummoxed me,' he said, 'was how you knew how to make that television go wrong. You never used to be much good with machines.'

'Easy,' said Victoria, smiling happily. 'I just twiddled all the knobs in turn. They were too busy looking at the picture to notice what the knobs were doing.'

Albert rose from his chair and walked thoughtfully around the room, stroking his moustache, then he took out his pocket watch, said 'Ah!' and announced: 'It's Christmas Eve, my dear. We have only a few hours left to achieve our purpose. Come, let's see if we can spoil someone's beauty sleep . . .'

Upstairs, Aunt Prudence lay wrapped in dreams, her lilac hair encased in a net and her mouth trembling slightly as she breathed out with little pop-pop-popping snores.

'The window,' whispered Albert, gliding over to it and lifting the catch. In a moment, an icy wind was shifting the curtains and playing around the bed. Aunt Prudence moved sleepily and pulled the covers high over her neck.

Victoria, unseen at the foot of the bed, immediately gave a little tug, and the covers once more

39

slipped down. With a grunt, Aunt Prudence pulled them up again. Up and down, up and down they went, while the room became colder and colder. A gentle twitch, to one side this time, and the eiderdown slid to the floor.

With a moan of annoyance, Aunt Prudence sat up and rubbed her eyes. Seeing the window open, she heaved herself out of bed and waddled over in her salmon-pink nightgown to close it. Then, muttering crossly, she climbed back into bed and heaved herself on to one side, hugging the bedclothes to her chin. Soon, she was once more snoring.

'Right?' whispered Victoria.

'Right.'

While Albert once more unlatched the window, Victoria slowly and carefully untucked the covers from the foot of the bed and rolled them back so that Aunt Prudence's fat pink toes would feel the full benefit of the wintry draught.

'Sweet dreams!' they whispered, and then they were gone.

In the morning Mrs Wetherby looked up from the stove as Aunt Prudence came into the kitchen. 'Sleep well?' she asked brightly.

Aunt Prudence settled herself at the kitchen table. 'I most certainly did not,' she said. 'That room has a faulty window catch, for a start, and the bedclothes are too small. My blankets were forever coming untucked. Then, this morning, I ran myself a hot bath – full to the brim, to warm myself up – but while I was fetching something from the bedroom, someone pulled out the plug. That Peter, if you ask me.'

'Oh dear, what a shame,' Mrs Wetherby said sympathetically, turning towards the stove so that Aunt

Prudence could not see her face. Serve the old bag right, she thought, for taking all the hot water. 'Never mind,' she went on. 'Have some porridge – that should make you feel better.' She began to ladle some porridge into a bowl, and at that moment, Mr Wetherby and the children came into the kitchen.

'Hurry up and sit down,' said Mrs Wetherby, turning away from the stove. 'Porridge, everyone?'

Aunt Prudence glanced menacingly at Peter, then inspected the bowl which Mrs Wetherby placed in front of her. 'Porridge, is it?' she asked, prodding it with her spoon. She helped herself to milk and sugar and gave it all a good stir. Then, her eyes narrowing with greed, she raised the spoon to her mouth.

What happened next was so quick that no one was quite sure afterwards how it had all come about.

With a gurgling cry, Aunt Prudence pushed away her porridge bowl and jumped to her feet. Unfortunately, Danny's skateboard had somehow found its way under the table, and Aunt Prudence's feet, landing on it, shot forward, causing her to fall. As she fell, she clutched at the tablecloth, and so ended up slumped on the floor, drenched in orange juice and milk, with a pot of marmalade in her lap and a bowl of porridge upside down on her head.

. . . Of course, she wouldn't stay a moment longer. Definitely not. She was off to Mildred's in Bournemouth. There was still time to get a train, thank goodness. As Mr Wetherby got the car out, ready to drive her to the station, the rest of the family gathered by the front door.

'Goodbye, Aunt Prudence,' they said, one after the other. 'We're so sorry . . .'

With a loud sniff, and toss of her porridge-damp curls, she was gone, and the sound of the departing car was lost in the shouts of glee.

'Good riddance!' yelled Peter.

'Bad rubbish!' bellowed Danny.

'Merry Christmas!' said Wendy.

'Wasn't it odd,' said Mrs Wetherby, 'how everything went wrong for her. She seemed to be haunted by bad luck.'

'Not at all,' Wendy replied. 'She brought it all on herself.'

Up in the spare bedroom, now mercifully free of Aunt Prudence's belongings, Albert and Victoria sat on the bed, laughing till the tears slid down their misty cheeks.

'All that pepper in her porridge . . .' chuckled Victoria. 'And the skateboard – oh, the skateboard!'

'We did it,' said Albert, leaning lazily back against the pillows. 'We actually did it. And they didn't suspect a thing. Now we can all have a really jolly Christmas. I think perhaps we might join the family for their Christmas dinner . . . watch them pulling crackers, putting on their funny hats – not so's they'll notice us, of course,' he added hurriedly.

Victoria had risen from the bed and was wandering about the room. 'Albert,' she said quietly, 'look at the curtains . . .'

Although the window appeared to be firmly closed, the curtains were moving, as if stirred by a breeze. A strangely familiar chill seemed to rise from floor level.

Albert sat up. 'What on earth . . . ?' he said.

There was a strong smell of wintergreen, and then a tall, slim form slowly took shape in the middle of the room. A long, dark grey dress, spectacles on a chain, a face as sharp and cold as a chisel.

'Oh m-m-my!' gasped Victoria.

'Hell's bells!' cursed Albert. 'It's Great Aunt Isobel!'

42

The figure spoke. 'Albert . . . Victoria . . .' it said, in a voice reminiscent of a chalk squealing across a blackboard, 'how very nice to see you. I thought I would give you a pleasant surprise. I've come to stay – for Christmas.'

ISOBEL'S PONY
Christine Pullein-Thompson

'You do remember the children, don't you?' asked Mummy on our way to the station. 'We all met at the British Museum when you were quite small. Clara bought you a packet of fudge.'

I nodded. Clara was Mummy's cousin.

'Shall I call her Aunt Clara?' I asked. There was a knot in my stomach. I hated leaving home, but, most of all, I hated leaving my dun pony, Crispin.

'Yes, and call George, Uncle George. It sounds more polite. I expect Clara will meet you at Meadowhill. And *remember* – don't talk to strange men on the train.'

We had reached the station. Mummy had made me wear a skirt, which I had topped by my favourite sweater which was orange with a polo neck.

My train was waiting. 'Have a good time,' said Mummy, kissing me goodbye. 'And don't worry. Uncle George and Aunt Clara are very kind.'

'Say goodbye to Crispin for me,' I answered, though I had said goodbye to him three times already. 'I hope he will be all right. I hope Mr Chambers will remember to check his water. I hope he doesn't get laminitis. I hope . . .'

But now the train was pulling out of the station and Mummy was getting smaller and smaller, until at last I could see her no longer.

I shut the window and tried to read a book, but I couldn't concentrate. I had never been away on my

44

own before and I kept wondering what would happen if Aunt Clara and I failed to recognize each other. Or if I alighted at the wrong station. Or if I hated her children. Or, worse still, they hated me.

Meadowhill station was small and bathed in sunlight when I reached it, I could not see Aunt Clara anywhere. I stood on the platform trying to keep calm, holding my small suitcase. The ticket collector eyed me anxiously. A puppy, nailed down in a crate, whined. Outside, birds sang.

'There she is!' shouted a voice, and two boys dashed into the station while behind them a girl called, 'Wait, don't we need platform tickets?'

They had long hair and wore jeans and tee shirts.

'Isobel Browne?' said the eldest. 'Here, let me take your case.'

The girl was dressed in the same way, but her hair was longer still.

'I was looking for Aunt Clara,' I said.

'Well, we'd better introduce ourselves,' said the largest boy. 'I'm Larry. This is Paul, and this odd-looking female is called Patricia.'

'Shut up, beast,' replied Patricia, aiming a kick at him.

I remembered them as small in fitted coats and with short, brushed hair. In those days they had had a nanny. They had been meek and polite, wearing patent leather shoes and white ankle socks.

'Sorry about the old bus,' said Larry now, opening the door of a battered car. 'The old man won't subscribe to anything better.'

'Larry gets through a car a month,' said Paul.

'Did you have a good journey?' asked Patricia.

'Yes, thank you.' I felt small and out of place, and idiotic in my skirt.

Their house looked across a small, tumbling river

to wooded hills. Beside it stood the remains of a castle.

I looked hopefully in the fields for ponies, but there were none. Larry parked the car in front of the house and kicked off his shoes.

'Patricia will show you your room,' he said, throwing my case at his sister.

She caught it and, saying 'Beast!' again, led me barefoot up a wide flight of stairs. 'He's mad,' she said. 'It's very sad. Where have your parents gone?'

'Rumania and Hungary. Daddy's selling agricultural machinery. It's the first time Mummy's gone with him,' I replied.

'Lucky them.'

My bedroom window looked across the remains of the castle to the tree-shadowed river. Once the castle must have dominated that particular stretch of the river completely; now only some of its outer walls remained, while, inside, thistles grew. I imagined knights stepping out of boats, the peaceful splash of oars. Patricia put my case on a chair.

'Did anyone tell you anything about this place?' she asked, looking at me anxiously. 'I mean, are you nervous? Do you get upset easily?'

'I don't know. I don't think so. It depends. I would be upset if Crispin died, or Mummy, or Daddy.'

'Of course,' replied Patricia impatiently. 'Well, I suppose there's no point in beating about the bush; but I wish Daddy had told you before you came.'

'What?' I was beginning to feel alarmed. 'About what?'

'About our ghost?'

'What sort of ghost?' I could feel the hair standing up along my back, but when Patricia said, 'It's a pony,' all my alarm vanished.

46

'Or it may be a horse, I don't know. It's grey, anyway,' she continued.

'Well, I don't mind a horse. I love them. I've got a pony of my one.'

'That's all right then,' said Patricia, sounding relieved. 'The poor animal is looking for something. It only comes at this time of the year and is utterly harmless. See you at dinner; it's in ten minutes. Owly beats a gong.' She ran out of the room slamming the door after her.

I sat on my bed, suddenly homesick. Patricia and her brothers have thought up this ghost to frighten me, I thought. What wonderful hospitality! But I'm not going to be frightened, I decided, washing my hands. I'm going to sleep like a top. Wishing that I was as tall and arrogant as my cousins, I put on my oldest pair of jeans. Then a gong boomed and someone called, 'Isobel, it's dinner.'

Aunt Clara and Uncle George sat at different ends of the large dining-room table. They stood up to shake hands with me. It was all horribly formal. I was made to sit on Uncle George's right because I was a guest. Owly waited at table as she had apparently for the last twenty years. She wore spectacles – which only partially hid large, owl-like eyes – a black dress and a plain white apron. She called me 'Miss Isobel'. I used my dessert spoon for my soup and mixed up my knives. Aunt Clara and Uncle George talked to me about agricultural machinery – of which I know nothing. If they had talked about Crispin and the pony club, everything would have been all right; as it was, dinner for me was a small social disaster.

Afterwards Patricia suggested a game of Monopoly and we played until bedtime, sitting at a table

47

in the hall, while Paul sat on the stairs playing his transistor at full volume.

When I retired to bed, I found the curtains drawn and my pyjamas waiting for me on my pillow. The rest of my clothes had been unpacked and put away. I was suddenly very tired. The morning seemed to belong to another life.

Patricia came in to say goodnight. 'Don't worry about footsteps in the night,' she said. 'The boys stay up for hours.'

'I won't,' I answered, getting into bed.

'Is everything all right?' she asked next, glancing round the room. 'Has Owly given you enough towels, soap, everything?'

I nodded. I felt very far from home, and I much preferred my own more humble bedroom with pictures of horses pinned to the walls and my few rosettes above my bed.

'And remember, if you hear a neigh or two in the night, it's just our ghost. Nothing to worry about. A few more weeks and he will be gone until next summer.'

'I shall certainly look out if I hear a neigh,' I answered. 'I've always wanted to see a ghost. But if it's one of your awful brothers pretending, I shall be absolutely furious. In fact I shall throw something at him.'

'They're not that mad,' replied Patricia, laughing before she left.

I lay in my luxurious bed and, being too tired to read, switched off my elegant bedside light. Moonlight filtered through the curtains, a light wind stirred the trees outside. I could hear Paul's transistor still playing in the distance; otherwise everything was quiet. I wondered whether Crispin had missed my usual evening visit and whether my parents had landed in Bucharest yet. Somewhere in the house a clock chimed ten times. I thought I heard Uncle George saying goodnight to someone. Then a door slammed and there was silence. After that I must have slept, though I cannot remember falling asleep. I know I dreamed that Crispin had escaped from the orchard and that he was neighing. He walked up and down below my window and then he neighed again and this time it was like a call for help. He seemed to be crying, 'Come, please come.'

And then I was sitting up in bed, sweating, knowing that it wasn't a dream any more, that there really was a pony outside calling to me in the moonlight. My heart started to beat in an idiotic manner. It's the ghost, I thought. Patricia wasn't joking after all. There really is one!

I stepped out of bed on to shaky feet, and a minute must have passed before I found the courage to draw back the curtains and look out.

The moon was partly covered by a cloud, but I could see the pony clearly standing alone in the long grass by the castle. He was looking up, his eyes searching for something or someone. He wore the sort of tack ponies wore long ago, including a saddle which was stained with something that looked like blood. His head was small, set on a fine arched neck, and he shook a long blood-soaked mane before he trotted away like a dancer without looking back.

My teeth were chattering now. I was suddenly certain that I had seen the pony somewhere before. But where? And when? It was obvious he had existed years and years ago; so how could I know him? But the feeling remained and I had difficulty in stopping myself from going down to him. I wanted to put my arms around his poor neck, to comfort him, to say . . . to say what? The words were there, some pet words in the back of my brain, which belonged to him. I'm going mad, I thought. I don't know the pony. I can't. Tears were running down my face now. I opened the window, but the pony had vanished. And now the first of the birds was singing and, above the river, dawn was breaking.

I returned to my bed. So Patricia *wasn't* joking, I decided, putting on the light. There is a ghost. And I know him! Somehow, somewhere, we have met. 'But you know that is impossible, Isobel, you fool,' I told myself. 'He belongs to the days of knights. He's a palfrey. How could you, for pity's sake. Where's your sanity?'

But sanity and reason had nothing to do with it. It was beyond and above such things. I was attracted to him by something far stronger than either, and now my brain seemed to be going round and round in a mad circle, saying, 'I want to go to him, I want to go.' And I felt as though I was floating across the room and out of the window, as though some great force was dragging me, something I had no hope of withstanding. And then I was crying, 'I don't want to go, I don't want to,' and Patricia was shaking me and saying, 'It's me, Patricia.' And I didn't know where the hours had gone, for morning had come and the room was full of sunlight.

'Are you all right?' asked Patricia anxiously, peering into my face. 'You look awful.'

'As though I've seen a ghost, no doubt,' I said, trying to laugh.

'Did you?'

'Yes.'

'It's ten o'clock. We couldn't wake you. I've been up here five times.'

'He neighed twice,' I explained. 'I saw him. He's grey.'

'That's what he always does. I ignore him now. I think he's a bore, really. But then I'm not crazy about horses,' said Patricia, who was looking very healthy this morning. 'You weren't frightened, were you?'

'Of course not,' I lied bravely, trying to forget the horrors of the night. 'I shall be able to tell everyone at school about it. None of them has ever seen a ghost.'

'Well, get up then, lazy bones,' cried Patricia. 'We're going sight-seeing today.'

Breakfast was still waiting for me in the dining-room. Aunt Clara was reading a newspaper. She looked up at my approach.

'I hear our ghost came again last night. I hope he didn't worry you. He's quite a friendly ghost really,' she said.

'He's super,' I answered breezily, helping myself to cornflakes. 'What happened to him? Why does he come?'

'It's a long story and rather a sad one,' replied Aunt Clara. 'I think it might upset you.'

'I don't mind,' I replied, though I could feel a lump rising in my throat already.

'I'll tell you one day, but not this morning,' answered Aunt Clara, returning to her newspaper. 'It's too sad for such a lovely day.'

We looked round the local museum in the morning and, after a cold lunch, Patricia taught me to row on the river. It was one of those golden summer days which, looking back, seem to have had no beginning and no end. I was not very successful at rowing. My restless night had left its mark. My arms felt weak and lifeless and sometimes I felt as though I was a spectator looking at us both from a long way off. It was an eerie sensation. We were too late for tea when we returned to the house, but dinner was formal again, with Owly waiting on us. Aunt Clara stared at me with some consternation as I sat down.

'Are you all right, Isobel?' she asked. 'You don't look very well to me. Did our ghost upset you last night? Would you like to have Patricia's room? It's on the other side of the house.'

'No thank you. I'm quite all right,' I replied quickly, though now Uncle George and Aunt Clara both seemed to be fading into the distance.

'Oh dear, I do hope you're not going to be ill,' exclaimed Aunt Clara, growing smaller and smaller every second.

'Give her some water,' said Uncle George. 'Hurry.'

'I'm quite all right,' I said, as they came into focus again. 'I don't need water. It's just that I keep hearing hoof-beats and someone crying. . . .'

'Oh dear!' said Aunt Clara. 'What are we going to do?'

'Nothing. They've gone. I'm quite all right,' I answered, spooning soup into my mouth.

The boys had gone out to a party. After dinner, Patricia and I watched television in the small sitting-room by the kitchen which had once been the servants' hall. Aunt Clara popped her head round the door from time to time to ask, 'Are you all right, Isobel dear? Quite all right? Are you sure?'

'Yes thank you,' I answered each time. 'I'm fine.'

When we retired to bed, she gave us each a cup of Ovaltine. Mine had two sugar lumps on the saucer and I put them in my dressing-gown pocket.

'Are they for the ghost?' asked Patricia, watching me. 'Because he won't eat them. He fades away at the least sound. The boys tried to make friends with him years ago, but he just faded away into the shrubbery with one last, desperate neigh. If you're

52

scared, come into my room. Wake me up. I shan't mind. Promise.'

'All right, I promise.' I wanted to be alone now, for I felt as though I had an important appointment which I must keep at all costs.

'Goodnight,' I said. 'Sleep well. See you tomorrow.'

I opened my window and leaned out. Everything was still and beautiful; almost too beautiful for the heart to bear. There was hardly a ripple on the river, and the sky was darkening into night. It was easy to imagine the castle as it had been – full of people, with knights coming and going, and a great fire in the hall, horses being led away to stables, the clank of armour. I left the curtains undrawn and climbed into bed, and I must have fallen asleep immediately, for right away I started to dream that I was riding a grey pony. I sat sideways in a long skirt with a groom following on a big horse. Everything was extremely vivid, not blurred nor muddled as dreams so often are. The trees were green with leaves and there were flowers everywhere. I had a feeling of intense happiness, as though suddenly all my dreams were coming true.

I was humming a tune when the neigh rang out, and I sat up in bed instantly, because I had known all along that it would come, that my appointment was with the grey pony outside – whether I wanted it or not. I still wore my dressing-gown and my legs carried me unasked out of the room and down the wide stairs. My hands knew how to draw back the bolts on the door into the garden. The grass was wet with dew and there was a smell of roses which I had not noticed before.

The grey pony stood just where he had the night before, his ears pricked, his eyes searching for me, and now I was running, tripping over the lawn, wrenching open the iron gate. I no longer wore my pyjamas and dressing-gown, but a long skirt which reached to my ankles, a cloak, and a hat with a feather in it.

'Silver!' I cried. 'Silver!' And the pony whinnied, recognizing me at once, and all the misery left his eyes. He came towards me as a friend, his nostrils nickering. I held out my hand, with the sugar in it.

I felt his whiskers brush against my fingers, his breath on my hand. Then he gave a loud sigh, a sigh of pure contentment. The sort of sigh one might give when one had reached home after a long and arduous journey. And then, without warning, everything changed; Silver was gone and I was fighting for my life with a cloak over my head. I tried to scream, but no words would come and I knew now without doubt that I was dying, falling into space, into nothingness, and I didn't want to die. And then there was darkness, silent and absolute, and I knew that this was the end . . .

'He knew me,' I said.

I felt as though I had been away for a long time and come back. Mummy was sitting at the end of my bed, wearing her navy blue suit.

'She's coming round!' she exclaimed.

Aunt Clara was sitting in a chair. Sunshine streamed through the cracks in the drawn curtains.

'How did you get here?' I asked, sitting up. 'What's the time? Is it Sunday or Monday?'

'It's Wednesday, darling,' replied Mummy, bending forward to kiss me.

'Give her some water,' said Aunt Clara. 'Here, take the glass.'

'He knew me,' I announced again, without really

meaning to, rather as a record keeps saying the same thing when the needle is stuck. I drank some water. It had ice in it. 'There was blood on his neck. It wasn't a dream, was it?' I asked. 'It did really happen, didn't it?'

'Of course, darling,' replied Mummy in a soothing voice, the sort of voice one might use to a very small child.

'We found you lying by the castle,' added Aunt Clara. 'Patricia was anxious, so she went outside to look.'

'He was alive because he took the sugar. Is it the same day?' I asked. 'The morning after.'

'No, you've been delirious for two days,' replied Mummy. 'I came back to be with you. Don't talk too much.'

'I'm so sorry,' I answered.

'It wasn't your fault, darling.'

'He hasn't been back. I don't think he will ever come back again,' said Aunt Clara.

'He knew me. How did he know me?' I asked slowly. 'He whinnied to me. He took the sugar.' Everything was suddenly crystal clear. 'He took the sugar,' I repeated. 'I know he did. I felt his whiskers.'

'Don't get excited,' said Mummy.

'We know he took the sugar,' Aunt Clara told me. 'Patricia searched for it. She looked in your pockets, too.'

'Rest, darling,' said Mummy. 'Lie back. Doctor Perkins will be here again soon.'

'I will get you something to eat,' said Aunt Clara, tiptoeing from the room.

I felt weak, but happy, too, in a strange exhausted way. I felt as though I had accomplished something of great importance. Silver's all right now, I thought. He's found peace at last. And I'm going to be all right, too. I'm not even mad and I can move all my limbs and open and shut my eyes and everything works!

Doctor Perkins was tall and dark. He took my pulse and temperature. He looked into my ears and eyes with a torch. He asked me to look in different directions, and knocked my knees with a little hammer.

'We could X-ray her skull,' he said, sounding perplexed.

'She seems quite well now – quite her usual self in fact,' replied Mummy.

'A spontaneous recovery,' said Doctor Perkins. 'But keep her quiet for the next twenty-four hours. I will call again tomorrow, unless you're worried.'

Aunt Clara showed him out.

'I'm all right,' I said. 'Why can't I get up? I'm sick of bed. I want to go outside.'

'Well, you can't,' said Mummy. 'Anyway, don't you want to hear the story?'

'What story?'

'Silver's, of course.'

'How do you know it?' I was sitting up again now, tense with excitement.

'It belongs to Isobel, too,' answered Mummy. 'Aunt Clara told me it yesterday when you were delirious. I think the two Isobels were fighting over you, but thank goodness, my Isobel won.'

Aunt Clara had returned with a tray covered with cups and saucers and plates, bread and butter, jam, three kinds of cake and a pot of tea with sugar and milk.

'You tell her about Silver, Clara. You will tell it better than me,' said Mummy, pouring tea.

'Is she well enough?'

Mummy nodded. 'The colour is back in her

cheeks. You are feeling all right now, aren't you, Isobel?'

'Yes.' I took a piece of cake and waited while downstairs in the hall a clock chimed four times.

Patricia came into the room and sat down on a chair.

'It all happened a long time ago,' began Aunt Clara, as though she was reading from a book, and I could see it all in my mind; the ruined castle standing tall and brave with turrets at each end, a landing stage on the river, a flag flying.

'The house wasn't here, of course. Our ancestors lived in the castle – yours as well as ours, Isobel. The castle was big, with dungeons – '

'And turrets at each end,' I interrupted.

'Yes. I will show you a drawing of it later.'

'And Isobel came on her grey pony, followed by a groom. And there were a great many trees. She came through a forest.'

'How did you know?' asked Aunt Clara.

'I just do,' I replied.

'She had reared Silver from a foal. They were inseparable,' continued Aunt Clara. 'She was expecting a baby and her husband had inherited the castle. He was dead, but no one had told her.'

'This is the awful part,' said Patricia.

'He had died fighting in France. But she was expecting, and, if the baby was a son, he would inherit the castle.'

'So she was killed,' I cried. 'She was happy because she thought she was going to live in the castle with her husband. She thought his relations would welcome her.'

'But her uncle-in-law wasn't like that' said Aunt Clara. 'He had her brutally murdered when she

57

arrived on a dark September night, and they buried her and her servant where this house now stands.'

'He was our great, great, great uncle,' said Patricia, biting her nails.

'What about Silver?' I asked.

'They drove him away into the forest, but he kept coming back, so, in a fit of anger, they killed him. But he still came back each September, looking for Isobel.'

'Until three nights ago,' said Mummy.

'What no one at the castle knew was that Isobel already had a baby girl, your great-great-grandmother,' said Aunt Clara.

'I'm sure you haven't said enough greats,' exclaimed Patricia.

'And because of your relationship to her, you look like the first Isobel,' said Mummy.

'I don't just look,' I answered. 'I *was* her. I knew I had met Silver before, the moment I saw him. I've just been back through time. But he's all right now. He'll never come back.'

Soon after that I fell asleep again, and a day later Mummy and I left to join Daddy in Rumania. I have never returned to the house, but I write to Patricia from time to time, particularly around September, and she assures me that Silver has never been back.

THE LIFE AND SOUL OF THE PARTY
Julia Birley

Down in Penge where I live there used to be a huge dilapidated church, all pointed windows and grinning gargoyles. One day the surveyors came to look round and make plans to knock it down and build a new one. Mr and Mrs Cox, who lived close by, saw them out of their front window as they sat sorting prizes for the Parish Children's Party. They had quite an argument. Mr Cox was attached to the old St Ethelburga's. His wife decidedly was not.

'It's just a useless bit of run-down Victorian gothic. A regular rocky horror. People throw their litter into the graveyard. It gives me the creeps.'

'But it's got character. It's got traditions,' insisted Mr Cox, who was romantic. 'Those Victorians were a dynamic lot. They thought big. Look at the Crystal Palace – '

'How can I? It was burnt down.'

'But can't you imagine it – all glittering? The fountains, the marbles – my word, if they could see what it looks like now!'

'It's enough to make them rise from their graves,' Mrs Cox agreed. 'And not only the buildings. Look at the way kids behave nowadays. I can tell you I'm dreading this party in the Church Hall. Wish we'd never got roped in for it.'

'We could certainly do with a spot of Victorian discipline. Especially when Larry Murdoch and that

59

young Trevor get going. Now when St Ethelburga's was first built, people had ways of dealing with infant greasers. They were seen and not heard.'

'I dare say it will be all right,' Mrs Cox said. 'So long as you manage to keep them running about.'

Mr Cox did not feel too sure of that, as he went over to the church next day about an hour before the kick-off. The Parish ladies had been busy, putting holly round the door and Chinese lanterns all along the dark south aisle, which led through to the lighted hall where the party was to be. But it would have taken more than that to cheer up St Ethelburga's. The prim, tall pillars, the black vaults overhead and the smell of musty hymn books all seemed to say: How dare you? What is the meaning of this disgusting frivolity? Mr Cox shivered slightly, and just then something butted him from behind. Several children, arrived much too early, went stampeding past to the hall, their innocent faces aglow as they barged against each other with gleeful yells. Mr Cox went after them, feeling tired already.

Just inside the hall, he caught the two worst boys nicking sausage rolls from the buffet. 'Understand,' he said, grabbing Trevor by the collar. 'I want no funny business from either of you this evening.'

Trevor rolled his eyes and smirked. 'I dunno what you mean.' His mate Larry belched and blew crumbs all over Mr Cox, who prayed silently for help. To anything that would listen.

Already, as they say in the papers, the situation was deteriorating. Someone struck up on the tinkly piano for musical bumps, but the children were too excited to play properly. Those who were out refused to stay out, and tried to clobber the rest. By six o'clock, when the party was really due to start, Mrs Cox (who was supposed to be pouring the drinks) was mopping the nose of a sobbing victim. She was muttering rude things about her husband for not keeping better order. Just then a buzz went round among the grown-up helpers. The conjurer had arrived, and was waiting in the church.

'What conjurer? Never knew we'd engaged a conjurer – ' But Mr Cox said: 'All I know is, Mafeking has been relieved.' Then he bawled for silence, and told the children to sit on the floor, as he had a surprise for them. Trevor, Larry and their gang shoved to the front. In the pointed doorway, a black figure was silhouetted against the faint glow from the lanterns. He beckoned it forward. The children raised a few cheers and cat-calls, the helpers clapped eagerly.

They saw a long, thin figure, dressed in an outfit that might have been hired from a theatre: frock coat, clerical collar, tall hat, white gloves, luxuriant ginger whiskers. He was wheeling a porter's trolley, which held a domed trunk of gleaming leather, with new brass handles, and 'MAGIC' boldly painted on the lid.

It seemed to take the conjurer no time to reach the platform. There he turned and smiled down the hall in a vague, fixed way. Between the improbable whiskers, his face was very pink and white. The smile never left it, as he intoned in a sing-song tenor:

'Will someone assist me to elevate my magic box?'

The mob jostled round, and the trunk almost floated up by itself. Its owner bounded after it, with his arms folded, like a ballet dancer. The kids laughed and whistled, but some looked a little unnerved.

'If only his tricks are as good as he is,' prayed Mr Cox. 'At least he's got them on his side.'

But he spoke too soon. All the time this mystery conjurer was opening his trunk and taking out his

61

stock-in-trade, the usual wand, scarves, goldfish bowl, folding screen and the like, the mobsters in the front row sniggered and scuffled. The first few card tricks were rather familiar. Larry kept explaining loudly how each one was done, while the others blew raspberries, or mimicked the conjurer's voice, which was certainly peculiar. The next row told them to belt up, whereupon they swivelled round and began to use their boots. Mr Cox rolled up his sleeves. He'd hoped he wouldn't have to throw anybody out, but it seemed the time had come. Then an odd little headshake from the platform made him pause.

'For the next trick,' smiled the conjurer, 'I require two volunteers. For disappearing.'

Some dear little girls stood up, but too late. Trevor and Larry had rushed the platform, more as if they were going to attack the conjurer than help him. Calmly he opened the trunk and bowed an invitation. They hesitated only for a moment. Then:

'Come on,' said Trevor. 'Let's bust 'is box for 'im an all.'

'Watch me, here I come!' shrieked Larry.

They both jumped in heavily. Clearly they had no idea of allowing the lid to be shut on them. But something happened – whether they sank or were forced down, the audience could not see – but the conjurer was doing up the strap. He turned away, dusting his gloved hands, and began a series of quite brilliant tricks. The children were rivetted. They shouted: 'Go on, Mister. Do another.' Then, after about ten minutes, one of the front row stood up and asked, in a respectful tone such as he had probably never used before, if Larry and Trevor could come out now, please?

'Bless my soul, I almost forgot.' The conjurer opened the trunk, looked surprised, then tipped it towards the audience. Of course it was empty – an empty black cavern. Both children and grown-ups clapped frenziedly. Only Mr Cox looked gloomy. He was certain that those boys would now emerge, leering, from somewhere quite different, under the platform or behind the curtain.

'Stop a minute, here's someone!' Their entertainer stooped and lifted out two rabbits, which he gave to the dear little girls. 'Will these do?'

'YES!' roared the audience.

'No,' protested some of the front row.

'One moment. Here are some more.' Out came a kitten, a puppy, a flock of doves. Out came a small alligator – which he hastily dropped into the piano. Out came toys, rather good ones, for all the children. Little flames danced at the ends of the conjurer's fingers. He lifted his hat, and it rained chocolate drops. Then, bowing briefly, he tossed his equipment back into the trunk, and leapt from the platform.

'Now for tea,' he cried. 'And then some jolly games.'

After this, the Blind Man's Buff, the guessing games and the dancing went like clockwork. The conjurer seemed to be everywhere at once, his black legs working like scissors, his whiskers flying. No one noticed how the time was going until the caretaker appeared at the door, rattling his keys. The conjurer was prancing round the hall, astride an old mop, with the whole party following and joining in the chorus of some ancient song:

'Hey, hey, clear the way, here comes the Galloping Major!'

Mr Cox stood looking on and wiping tears of laughter from his eyes. It was the best party he ever remembered. Suddenly his arm was disagreeably pinched, and a voice snarled: 'Where's my Larry?'

It was Mrs Murdoch, flashily dressed and flinty-faced, who seemed to be in a bad temper. 'One of his mates came to fetch me. I was just having a drink with some friends. He said you'd sent him off somewhere. Well, I paid 10p for his ticket. He should be here.'

Mr Cox said: 'Oh dear.' He supposed the joke had gone far enough. He went up to the conjurer, who suddenly turned and headed for the platform. Mr Cox stopped just where he was, and everything went black for a moment.

For he had been close enough to see that mask-like face sideways for the first time. And it really was a mask. The rim was visible behind the ear, and just above where the whisker began was a narrow gap. In that gap was – nothing.

When his sight cleared, the trunk was open. Trevor and Larry were scrambling out. He saw them slink down from the platform, both rather pinched and blue, as if with cold. Larry ran up to his mother and flung his arms round her. 'Let's go home, Mum,' he pleaded.

'Here, don't do that. Mind my good suit. What's the hurry? Didn't you enjoy the party?'

'Oh, yes, thank you, Mum – ' His teeth chattered a bit. Then he caught Mr Cox's eye, and dropped his gaze hurriedly. 'And thank you too, Mr Cox.'

Trevor couldn't bring himself to say anything, but he shook hands, earnestly, for several seconds.

Wherever those boys had spent their evening, Mr Cox was heartily glad he hadn't been with them.

Meanwhile the hall had almost emptied. The tall-hatted figure stood near the door, patting the last little heads as they went out. The thought of what might be inside those patting gloves turned Mr Cox rather sick. But he felt that he had had a lesson in

minding his manners, and certainly someone ought
to say thank you to – it.

But even as he hastened towards the door, the
conjurer vanished into the church. The lanterns had
mostly burned out, and the shadows hung over him,
black and powerful. 'Stop – er, stop a moment,' he
called waveringly. There were footfalls – oh, how he
hoped they wouldn't turn back – and he caught the
whisper of a song:

'Hey, hey – clear the way – '

He screwed up all his courage and ran along the
aisle with a thumping heart. Here was the open
church door, and the friendly street lamps. No one
was in sight. Just the mass of the church against the
sky, and the grave, stones that seemed to nod a little
in the night wind.

'Excuse me, Mr Cox – ' called the caretaker,
making him jump. He went back to the hall, where
the clearing up was almost finished.

The old man was grumbling. 'Now, sir, I must
ask you to give me a hand with this here trunk. Why
it should have been dragged out of the vestry and all
the way along here into the hall, beats me. The vicar
wouldn't half be wild if he knew – '

The trunk was very old, battered and dusty.
Nothing was written on the lid. The caretaker swore
it had lived in the vestry as long as he could remember. There was nothing inside but a few dead spiders.

During the next few weeks, a lot of people asked
Mr Cox how he had got hold of the marvellous
conjurer. He found he couldn't tell them the truth.
After all, he was a bank manager, with a reputation
to keep up, and he didn't want them to think he was
mad. So he pretended, even to his wife, that it was
just a local man who had rung up at the last minute

and offered to come. Unfortunately he hadn't given his address.

In the spring, the demolition company moved into the street, which echoed with the crash of falling masonry. St Ethelburga's vanished forever, and a lot of surprised-looking sky appeared in the gap.

Mr Cox felt sad. He went to the archives department in the local library and read up all he could about the church. His heart beat a little faster when he found an old Parish Magazine, with an account of a Ladies' Evening in 1882, presided over by the curate, the Reverend Francis Wherry. 'His humorous songs,' it said, 'will make him the life and soul of any party ever to be held in this hall.' Did he sing them 'The Galloping Major'? There was nothing about that. And if he was a conjurer as well, it didn't say so.

Disappointed, Mr Cox yielded to temptation at last, and confessed the whole story to his wife. But she wasn't much help either. She said she didn't remember enough to know if he was telling the truth, or had just dreamt it all, and the only merciful things about children's parties is the way you forget them.

At least Larry and Trevor were different boys ever afterwards. Everyone noticed it. When last I heard of them, both had joined the Venture Scouts, and were considered an ornament to their troop.

DREAM GHOST
Sydney J. Bounds

Mandy awoke suddenly in the night, trembling with fear. Moonlight flooded her bedroom with silver and shadow. It was only a dream, she told herself, only a dream. So why was she shivering in a warm bed?

A memory of the dream returned and she threw back the bedclothes and switched on the light. It had all seemed so real, and she'd never had a fright like that before.

She wrapped a dressing-gown around her and opened the door. The house was quiet, the passage in darkness, as she felt her way along the wall to her brother's room. She opened the door and closed it behind her, switched on the light.

Joe's room was full of aeroplane models, and she had to move carefully to avoid them. She sat on the edge of his bed and shook him hard; Joe was a heavy sleeper.

Presently, her brother stirred, 'What's up, then? Mandy . . .'

'I had a nightmare, Joe. It scared me – I've got to talk to somebody.'

Joe was twelve, two years younger than his sister, and sturdy, with unruly fair hair.

Mandy shuddered. 'It was horrid!'

Joe sat up reluctantly; he was still sleepy. 'What was it about?'

'I was walking along, through a mist, and all round me were ruins. It was nowhere I've ever seen, I'm sure of that. And then *she* came towards me, through the mist. Her feet didn't touch the ground – she just drifted along. I could see right through her, Joe. She was a ghost, a girl of about my age in a long dress, and with a pale face. Her mouth was moving as if she was trying to say something, but I couldn't hear what it was – like watching the old silent movies on telly. That's all, really, because I woke up. But it was so real.' She forced a laugh. 'I don't know why I was scared so much – it was only a dream.'

Joe rubbed sleep from his eyes and looked hard at his sister. 'You do look a bit white . . . Still, I never heard of anyone dreaming a ghost before.' He sounded impressed.

Mandy stood up. 'I'll be all right now, Joe. Thanks for listening.'

She tiptoed back to her room, and it was a long time before she fell asleep.

A week later, Mandy dreamed again. She stood among the ruins of an old house and it was dark. The ghost girl appeared before her, rippling as if seen through water. She felt icy cold. The ghost drifted nearer and lifted an arm, reaching out a hand to touch her . . .

Mandy awoke abruptly, soaked with sweat, her heart thumping wildly. She pushed bedclothes into her mouth to stop herself screaming. It was ridiculous, she thought, scared silly by a dream . . .

At the breakfast table, her mother commented: 'You look off-colour, Mandy. Are you sleeping all right?'

Joe hastily swallowed a spoonful of cereal. 'Was it the dream again?'

Their father looked up from his newspaper crossword. 'What dream's this? First I've heard of it.'

'She dreamed a ghost,' Joe said proudly.

'A ghost?' Father looked interested. 'That's jolly original.'

Mother said, 'Well, don't do it again if it's going to make you ill.'

Mandy made a silent prayer that she would never dream that particular dream again. Ever.

Another week passed before the dream returned. This time Mandy was exploring overgrown shrubbery in the large garden surrounding the ruins. And when the ghost girl reached out a hand to touch her, the ground opened and Mandy fell into darkness. She was falling, falling . . .

She woke up screaming. The bedroom door opened and the light came on. Mother came in hurriedly, looking concerned.

'What is it, Mandy?'

'The dream,' she sobbed. 'The ghost came for me again!'

Mother put her arms around her, and gradually she quietened down. 'I'll leave the light on – and in the morning I'm taking you to see Dr Thomson. We can't have this going on any longer.'

Dr Thomson was a chubby little man with a red face and bushy grey hair. After he'd listened to Mandy's story, he admitted: 'This is a new one on me. Let's see now, you break up for the holiday soon – are you going away?'

'To Devon, to stay with an uncle. That's next week.'

'Not next week,' the doctor said briskly. 'Right now. Today. There's nothing like a change of air and a bit of exercise. Perhaps you've been studying too hard.'

At home, Father made a phone call while Mother packed two cases. Mandy and Joe got in the car, waving goodbye to Mother as they drove off.

Mandy began to feel better already as the car gathered speed on the main road to Exeter.

'It'll be fun,' Joe said. 'Uncle George and Ben and Polly. And Dartmoor to explore.'

Uncle George was an artist and designed sleeves for pop records; he was easy-going and the children could do what they liked. He was a widower and had only recently moved to a cottage on Dartmoor.

It was late afternoon when they arrived, driving across the desolate moor to a small cottage set beside a stream between hills. Pop music blared from a record-player. The children, Ben and Polly, came running out to greet them.

'Now we can have fun!' Ben shouted.

Mandy's father stayed for a meal before driving home, and Uncle George told him: 'She'll be all right here. A few days on the moor and she'll be too exhausted to dream. My two sleep like logs.'

It began to seem that Uncle George was right. In the days that followed, the four children explored the wild moor, hunting for bronze-age relics and barrows, chasing wild ponies, climbing the high tors. There was Devon cream for tea, and Mandy's skin turned nut-brown in the sun and wind; she felt fitter than she'd ever felt before – and the dream didn't come back to bother her.

Uncle George was at his easel, immersed in a new painting, and Polly and Mandy were cutting sandwiches. Ben announced: 'Today we're going to the old house for a picnic. It's a super place to play hide-and-seek.'

'O.K. kids,' Uncle George said absently. 'Mind you get back before dark.'

It was a bright sunny day when they set out, walking between ferns and yellow-flowering gorse. Ben, who had short legs and was inclined to be on the tubby side, complained: 'Not so fast.'

'Oh, come on Fatty!'

'Shut your face, Pretty Poll!'

Polly – who *was* pretty – ran ahead, blonde hair streaming. 'Can't catch me!'

The moor was empty of life except for some sheep in the distance.

'What's this old house?' Joe asked.

'It's not a house really, not any more. Just the ruins of one. But there are lots of walls standing, and thick shrubbery. No one ever goes there, so we'll have the place to ourselves.'

When they reached the ruins, all four were hungry, and Mandy and Polly set out their picnic lunch.

Mandy was finishing her sandwiches and drinking lemonade when she began to look around with fresh interest. She had the eerie feeling she knew this place; but that was impossible – she'd never been on Dartmoor before. The feeling persisted and the memory of her dream returned.

All at once she began to shiver. This was the place she'd dreamed . . .

Joe asked: 'Are you all right, Mandy?'

She nodded. 'It's just that this place reminds me of my dream. I'll get over it.' She jumped to her feet. 'Come on, let's play hide-and-seek.'

'I'll be seeker first,' Joe said.

Mandy and Ben and Polly ran off to hide while Joe shut his eyes and began to count to a hundred.

Mandy ran towards the shrubbery; it was thick and green with a lot of cover to hide in. Yet, as she approached, she felt curiously reluctant to enter the dark bushes. Behind her, Joe finished counting and called:

'Look out – I'm coming!'

Mandy took a deep breath and forced her way into the matted undergrowth. She moved slowly and quietly, and the green leaves closed above her head, shutting out the sun. She began to feel cold and lonely. She pressed deeper and deeper into the shrubbery, following what might once have been a path but was now grown over with weeds and wild flowers.

Far enough, Mandy thought – Joe won't find me here. She took a few more steps forward, and then . . .

Mist curled up from the ground in front of her and shaped itself into a human figure. Mandy stopped dead, her heart in her mouth. She was looking at the ghost girl of her dreams, a young girl wearing an old-fashioned frock. Her face was pale and her expression sad. The ghost wavered in the air before Mandy's staring eyes – and she could see dark green leaves through the wraith.

The ghost shimmered as it drifted towards her. Mandy stood paralysed, her legs turned to jelly. A slender arm was lifted and a hand reached out, touched her. The touch was as cold as ice, and it burned.

Mandy jumped. She turned and bolted in panic crashing through the bushes till she burst out into sunshine and collapsed on the grass.

Joe raced up, calling: 'Mandy! What's the matter?'

'The ghost, Joe . . . I saw her.' She pointed to the bushes. 'In there.'

'I'm going to look,' Joe said fiercely. 'I'll settle that old ghost.' He went into the shrubbery, determined, but moving warily.

Ben and Polly joined Mandy as Joe returned. He had a thoughtful expression on his face. 'I didn't see your ghost,' he said. 'What I did see was a dark, deep well. So it was lucky you did see her just then. We've got to tell Uncle George about this.'

Next day, Uncle George and a policeman visited the hidden well. At the bottom they found the skeleton of a young girl, which was later brought up and buried in the local churchyard.

How terrible, Mandy thought, to die like that.

She never dreamed of her ghost-girl again, though she tried. She would have liked the ghost to come back – just once – so she could thank the girl for saving her life. In a strange way, she knew she had lost a friend.

But Mandy never forgot her. She was reminded of her every time she looked at her wrist, at the marks that never completely faded – marks left where ghostly fingers had touched her.

DRESSED FOR THE OCCASION
by Terry Tapp

When Claire was asked by her best friend, Janet, if she would like to spend the Easter holiday at Talgar Castle, she did not hesitate for a second. 'Oh, I'd love to,' she said. 'Shall we write to our parents and ask if it will be O.K.?'

The two girls sat down to write the letters while the dormitory was still comparatively quiet. 'What's it like at Talgar Castle?' Claire asked, when they both finished. 'Do you have a butler and a cook and little French maids all dressed in black? It all sounds so terribly grand.'

'It is rather grand,' Janet replied seriously. 'We have a chauffeur, two stable boys, two gardeners and quite a number of menservants. Why, there must be at least fifty people working for us.'

'Really?' Claire asked.

'Oh, yes,' Janet said.

'Fifty people!' Claire tried to visualize what it must be like at Talgar Castle with so many people working there.

'Just keeping the servants fed is a major problem,' Janet continued. 'Then there are the gold plates to keep clean, and Mum has to have her jewels guarded day and night – ' A pillow flew through the air, hitting her on the shoulder.

'You devil!' cried Claire. 'You've been pulling my leg.'

'Well, you certainly asked for it,' said Janet. 'Actu-

74

ally, we took over Talgar because it was falling apart. Dad pays a very low rent because he has agreed to restore the interior of the castle.'

'So you don't even own it?'

'It's our home for as long as we want it,' explained Janet. 'Talgar was built on the site of an old castle, but it is really a manor house. It's built high up on a hill, surrounded by woods and fields, and there are two rivers which meet in the valley below us. I think it's the most beautiful place on earth.'

From the moment both girls' parents agreed that they could spend Easter together, time seemed to slow down to a snail's pace. Claire pestered Janet continually with questions about Talgar, and Mr Mooney, the assistant headmaster of the school, seemed intent on squeezing the last few drops of work from his unwilling pupils before reluctantly allowing them to start their holiday in earnest.

When the long-awaited day finally arrived, Claire was bursting with excitement. The journey to Talgar Castle was pleasant, and the smooth-running train wound through the picturesque countryside to arrive at the station punctually – an event which, Janet's father said later, should have been declared a miracle.

Mr Holly, Janet's father, was waiting for the girls in a mud-encrusted Land-Rover. Dressed in torn blue jeans and a thick, lumpy sweater, he wore a huge smile of welcome on his round face.

He took their suitcases as if they were filled with feathers, swinging them easily into the back of the Land-Rover.

'Your limousine awaits,' he said, bowing low and doffing his multi-coloured 'tea-cosy' hat. 'I came to fetch you personally because it is the chauffeur's day off and the Rolls-Royce is in the garage for its weekly polish.'

75

Claire giggled at that and Janet simply kissed her father lightly on the cheek and climbed up into the canvas-covered wagon as if it were a State Coach. 'Home, James,' she said imperiously.

They drove through the village with its rows of neatly thatched cottages, and Mr Holly chattered excitedly about the work he had been engaged upon. 'I still haven't done much with the second floor,' he told Janet, 'but the first floor is completed and the local council is very pleased with it. We were lucky enough to get some granite from the old market building when the council knocked it down for the redevelopment scheme, and they even delivered it to me free. Of course, we could do with a lot more help, but at the moment a housekeeper and a gardener are just about all we can afford.'

'So you *do* have servants,' Claire said to Janet. 'I thought you were kidding.'

'Don't let Mrs Billings hear you referring to her as a servant,' said Mr Holly with a mock look of terror. 'She would tear you apart, limb from limb.'

'I think Dad is a bit frightened of Mrs Billings,' said Janet.

'Who wouldn't be scared of old Bully Billings?' Mr Holly replied. 'Anyway, she bakes the most delicious pasties.'

He swung the car expertly around a sharp corner and started up the steep, winding hill towards Talgar Castle, which stood out against the grey sky like a frozen, granite giant. 'It's pretty bleak-looking,' Mr Holly admitted, 'but you'll like it once we get inside.'

The old Land-Rover grumbled up the hill, through the drive entrance and up to an archway which was set in the thick, wedge-shaped wall. Mr Holly drove carefully through the archway into the wide, cobbled yard, pulling the car up gently outside a tall, wooden door. Janet's mother had been watching out for them from the downstairs window, and when she saw the car arrive she rushed out to greet them warmly, ushering them into the vast, stone-floored kitchen, which was warm and steamy, smelling richly of cooked meat and onions. Claire watched as Janet hugged her mother and she felt, for the first time, a pang of loneliness for her own mother. But Mrs Holly came over and hugged Claire just as hard, and was so friendly that, within an hour of arriving, Claire felt as if she had known Janet's parents for a very long time indeed.

Mr Holly was a big, jovial man, intent on making the children laugh as much as possible, his own booming laughter being almost loud enough to make Talgar Castle shake in its foundations. Like a mother hen, Mrs Holly clucked around the children, filling them with fresh baked bread and ladlefuls of scalding hot soup which would, so she said, last them until supper time.

There was just enough time to explore the ground floor of the castle and change into casual clothes before Mrs Holly called them back into the kitchen for supper. Claire gazed in astonishment at the immense helping of meat and potatoes on her plate, thinking perhaps that she had been given Mr Holly's by mistake.

'Come on, girls,' said Mr Holly. 'Tuck in. Get yourselves outside of that. Plenty more vegetables in the tureens when you've polished that lot off.'

Claire, to her surprise, managed to clear everything on her plate and even ate two delicious helpings of home-made apple tart. Mrs Holly spooned thick cream as if it were custard, evidently delighted to feed such a big appetite.

When they had all eaten, Mrs Holly suggested that the girls looked around the castle for a while.

'That was a lovely meal, Mrs Holly,' said Claire. 'Shall we help with the washing up?'

Mrs Holly glanced from Claire's face to the pained expression on the face of her daughter. 'I don't think so,' she said. 'Do you usually wash up the dinner things when you are at home?'

'No,' said Claire. 'But I always offer when I'm a guest.'

'Come on,' Janet said. 'Let's see all the work Dad has been doing this term.'

'What she really means is that you had better go before I change my mind and ask you to help,' said Mrs Holly.

'That's right,' Janet said. 'Let's get out of here quickly.'

The girls ran laughing from the warm kitchen out into the great hall, from which there was access to several rooms, including a vast, oak-panelled room which was once, so Janet said, a ballroom. After exploring the ground floor thoroughly, they went up the wide, impressive stairway under the watchful eyes of the men and women who stared down from the oil-painted portraits. 'The paintings were here when we came,' Janet said. 'They don't belong to us. Mum is doing some research on them.'

'That one looks like old Moaney Mooney,' Claire said, pointing up at the picture of a bewigged man who was wearing an expression of absolute boredom.

'And this one looks like the Bride of Dracula,' said Janet. 'Funny – not one of the people in these portraits is smiling. Perhaps that's why we think the people in history books are such a dull, miserable lot.'

'Maybe people will look back on us and think we are grinning idiots,' Claire commented. 'Now we have photographs taken, instead of being immortalised in oils, and we always tend to smile at the camera.'

There were fourteen bedrooms on the second floor of Talgar Castle and another fourteen on the next floor up. 'Dad has roped the stairs off because he says it isn't safe to go up there until he has put new floorboards down,' explained Janet.

'What I don't understand,' said Claire, 'is why your parents want to live here at all. After all, there are far too many rooms for you to use. Doesn't it feel creepy living in such a vast place?'

'Creepy?'

'Yes, what with all those empty bedrooms above you and all these empty bedrooms on this floor – doesn't it make you feel creepy?'

'I've never really thought about it,' Janet said. 'The only thing which really does send shivers down my spine is the portrait of the old witch at the end of the landing.'

'Old witch?'

'That's what I call her,' said Janet. 'Come on, I'll show you.' Taking her friend by the hand, Janet led her to the end of the landing until they stood under a life-sized portrait of an exceedingly ugly old woman. The picture itself was thick with many coatings of varnish, but Claire could still just make out the colours of the woman's dress, which was profusely trimmed with Chantilly lace.

Examination of the woman's face showed Claire why Janet had referred to her as a witch. It was a grey, lifeless face; the skin was flaccid, wrinkled and hanging from the cheekbones in great sweeps, folding down from her slit mouth in heavy jowls. The expression on the woman's face was one of deep malevolence; the stony eyes were hard and black as pebbles. Claire felt an electric, tingling sensation along the back of her neck as she surveyed the portrait: never, in all her life, had she beheld such an evil countenance. 'She is horrid,' Claire whispered in awe.

'What are you whispering for?' Janet whispered back.

'I don't know,' said Claire. 'Come on, let's go back to the warm kitchen. That woman makes me feel cold.'

Once they were in the kitchen, Claire felt better. 'We were looking at the picture of the old witch,' she told Mrs Holly.

'Old witch?' Mrs Holly looked up from the newspaper she was scanning.

'She means the lady in the blue dress,' Janet explained. 'I call her an old witch because she is so ugly.'

'You mustn't call her that,' said Mr Holly. 'She'll come and haunt you if you're rude to her.'

'Really!' said Mrs Holly in a not unkind voice. 'You should know better than to get children excited just before bedtime.'

'Children don't believe in ghosts nowadays,' Mr Holly said. Then, looking at the children – 'I'm right, aren't I?'

Janet and Claire both shook their heads vigorously.

'Then perhaps it would be better to change the subject entirely,' said Mr Holly, smiling at the girls. 'How would you like to have a party next weekend?'

'A party!' Janet threw her arms around her father's neck in delight.

'To celebrate the completion of the first floor. I've invited one or two people from the council and some people from the village. We've been working so hard up here that we have hardly spared any time for social life. Now we intend to make amends.'

'Can it be a fancy dress party?' asked Janet.

'Oh, I don't know about that,' Mr Holly said.

'It isn't going to be all grown-ups and sherry and talking, is it?' asked Janet. 'Aren't we going to have some children up from the village? Susan Fielding would come, and there's Roger and Mary and–'

'What do you think?' Mr Holly said, raising his eyebrows at his wife. Mrs Holly smiled. 'I dare say we could have a fancy dress party if you want. I expect there are plenty of people who still have their costumes from last year's village carnival, and it should prove to be fun.'

They relaxed in the warm kitchen, talking about the party, and Claire was introduced to Mrs Billings, who had just returned from a day in town; it had been her half day off, but she seemed in no hurry to leave and discussed the party with them eagerly, making mouth-watering suggestions of chocolate cake and cream meringues.

'What a pity I didn't know about it,' said Claire. 'I haven't got a fancy dress costume.'

'Don't worry about that,' said Mrs Holly. 'We have a trunkload of clothes upstairs which we found when we turned out the attic here. I'm sure we can make something to suit you.'

They talked awhile, then Mrs Holly sent them off for a bath, after which Claire felt very tired and sleepy. She felt pangs of loneliness return as Mrs Holly tucked Janet up neatly and kissed her good-night, but when Mrs Holly did the same for her, she felt that she belonged to the family. Both girls were too tired to talk much as the excitement of the day caught up with them, and Janet slept the whole night through without stirring.

Claire would have slept well had not thoughts of the old woman intruded into her dreams. Somehow she could not get that cruel, malevolent face out of her mind. Out of the deep blackness of sleep there appeared that leering, chalky face, the cruel eyes penetrating like strong lights, almost dazzling Claire. The woman was laughing low, trembling with evil, inner delight, a smug expression twisting the grotesque features into a terrifying mask.

At one time during the night Claire had the impression that there was someone in the room, standing at the foot of the bed. It was too dark to make out a definite shape, but she was certain that someone was watching her through the inky darkness. And she thought she could hear breathing and the soft 'swishing' sound of a long skirt dragging along the floor. Sitting upright in the bed, her eyes filled with drowsy sleep, Claire could just make out the shape of a shimmering, luminous spectre. She reached out into the darkness, shrinking back as her hand touched something damp and cold. The vague shape started to solidify, forming a face and hands and arms.

Suddenly, Claire realized that it was the old woman.

She let out a scream, high pitched and piercing, filled with wild, terrifying panic, but no sound came from her lips. The apparition suddenly disappeared as if it had been switched off.

Janet slept soundly through all this and, as Claire was informed the next morning, so did everybody else in the house. In fact, after a good breakfast and lots of talk about the coming fancy dress party, Claire began to wonder if she had not dreamed it all. Mrs Holly had put it all down to an attack of indigestion, and Mr Holly had blamed himself for getting the girls so excited the night before. Mrs Billings reckoned that it was *her* fault for not being at Talgar to cook them a 'decent' dinner and that it was, indeed, some form of stomach upset. Mrs Billings had a deep suspicion of other people's cooking and considered herself, rightly so, the best cook for miles around.

Later that morning, Janet took Claire up to one of the bedrooms. Mr Holly came up to pull out an immense wooden trunk which was filled with dresses all crammed tightly together.

'Look – a boa,' Janet said, pulling out the long, feathery stole.

'I thought boas were snakes,' Claire replied.

'They are also feather stoles,' explained Janet, turning herself in a neat circle so that the frail white feathers wrapped themselves around her neck. 'I feel rather elegant in this.'

There were scores of dresses in the trunk, so the children amused themselves sorting through the pile, trying on various items and generally laughing at each other's antics.

'People were much smaller a hundred years ago,' said Janet knowledgeably, 'and that's why the clothes fit us. I think it's all the lovely food we get nowadays.'

When they had emptied the trunk, they sorted the clothing out into two piles. The children's dresses were very pretty, but far too small for Claire. One dress, in particular, attracted Claire's attention. It was very small, probably made for a six or seven-year-old, and made of pink and white checked woollen material with a plain pink silk veiling. There were two parasols, which were rather more ornamental than useful, and Janet's mother seemed delighted with the discovery of these, saying that they could very well be quite valuable as they were probably designed by Kate Greenaway. Then Janet came across a vaguely familiar-looking dress which was profusely trimmed with Chantilly lace.

'Isn't this the dress that the old woman is wearing in the portrait?' she asked.

Claire examined it reluctantly. Although she had now put last night's experience down to a nightmare, she certainly did not wish to be reminded of it again. 'I don't think so,' she replied off-handedly.

'I'm sure it is,' said Janet, gathering the dress in a rumpled heap and running from the room.

Claire followed her friend along the landing and watched as Janet held the dress up against the portrait. She was right. Although the many layers of varnish had almost obscured the true colouring of the dress, it was quite evident that the shape and style were exactly the same. 'It might be the actual dress the old witch was wearing when she sat for the portrait.'

'She was standing for the portrait,' Claire said.

'Even when you stand to have your picture painted they call it "sitting".' Janet said laughing. 'I don't know why that should be, but it's true.'

'It's a very pretty dress,' Claire said. 'It smells rather awful, but it's very elegant.'

'Let's ask Mum what she thinks,' said Janet.

The girls ran down to the kitchen, where Mrs Holly was busily peeling vegetables and Mrs Billings was rolling out a huge piece of pastry which was almost the size of the whole table top.

'Found something?' asked Mrs Holly.

She dried her hands, examined the dress critically and held it against Claire. 'Yes, it is about your size. People were much smaller in the old days.'

'I told you that,' said Janet.

'And I told *you* that,' Mrs Holly said. 'Old suits of armour were very small compared with the size of people nowadays, and you only have to look at the height of the doors in old cottages to get some idea of how small people were. Anyway, I think the dress will look very nice on you, Claire. What are you going to dress up as?'

'I think I'll be a Victorian woman,' Claire said.

'You can go as the old witch!' Janet burst out. 'Oh, wouldn't that be great? Dad could use some of his amateur acting make-up for your face, and you could have wrinkles and warts all over you.'

'But I –'

'And we've got an old wig upstairs.'

'But I don't want to be an ugly old witch,' Claire said. 'I want to be an elegant Victorian lady.'

'What a spoil sport!' Janet retorted. 'I think you'd make a smashing witch – and you wouldn't need much make-up either.'

Claire laughed at that, and Mrs Holly said: 'Claire must come as whatever she pleases. The main thing is that this dress will have to be dry cleaned. I'll send it this afternoon. It shouldn't take more than a couple of days.'

That evening, just for fun, Mr Holly decided that he would make Claire's face up so that she looked like the old woman. Working deftly with the cream and sticky grease paint, he managed to create a horrifying face which made Claire look even worse than the old witch in the portrait. They had so much fun that evening that Claire relented and decided that she would go as the old witch. 'It will certainly be original,' Mr Holly said. 'Anyway, I enjoy making people up.'

Some days later, when the dress had been collected

from the dry cleaner's shop in town, everyone agreed that it looked exactly like the one in the portrait. It was definitely a Victorian dress, and now that the ribbons and flounces had been properly arranged and ironed out, it looked as good as new. Claire was so excited by the appearance of the dress that she asked if she might try it on.

'I think that would be wise,' said Mrs Holly. 'If there are any alterations to be made, it would be as well to know in plenty of time.'

Claire ran quickly up the stairs to the bedroom that she and Janet were sharing, carrying the dress on its hanger so that it would not become creased. Pulling off her warm sweater and jeans she bunched the dress up gently in her hands and held it above her head.

It was like going into a tunnel; the dress was so thick that Claire could not see any light at all. She struggled to push her arms through the armholes and, as she tried to pull the dress down over her face, she felt the neckband tighten on her forehead. It was going to be a very tight fit indeed. Perhaps, she thought, I've got some of the ribbons twisted. Rather than tear the delicate material, she tried to remove the dress and start again. But the dress would not be moved. It seemed to have a mind of its own.

Claire tugged hard. It was getting very stuffy in that dark tunnel of material, and she imagined that she could feel the dress moving over her body. Something was terribly wrong. She panicked as she felt the dress move around her, pulling itself gently here, and gently there, easing itself on to her like a coiling snake. How she wished she had asked Janet to help her.

Suddenly her head popped out of the neckband into the bright daylight of the room, and when she looked down at herself she was surprised to see that the dress was fitting perfectly. Claire sat on the edge of the bed, exhausted after her efforts, wondering why such a comfortable dress should have been so difficult to put on. Examination of the ribbons and flounces revealed nothing. The dress fitted exactly. It might have been made for her. One thing was certain – she would have to get fully dressed before Mr Holly applied any make-up, otherwise it would all get scraped off when she put the dress on.

Opening the wardrobe door, Claire examined herself in the tall mirror. The length of the dress was perfect, and the ribbons flowed out beautifully. She stood sideways to admire the pleated flounces and the pointed panels of the bodice. It was a very fine dress indeed.

By chance she looked up at her face.

Her face!

She wanted to shout – scream . . . for the face which stared back at her was not her own!

The face which stared balefully back at her was that of the old woman in the portrait, red-rimmed eyes leering triumphantly at her, the mouth twisted grotesquely into an evil grin. Shuddering at the dreadful sight, Claire turned away from the mirror, fully expecting to see someone behind her. It *had* to be some sort of joke. There had to be an explanation.

'You fool!' The voice was loud and rasping with a cruel, malicious edge which made Claire return her astonished gaze to the mirror, where the image was now convulsed into laughter. 'You fool!' The old woman was shrieking now, the fleshy jowls rippling, exposing decayed, blackened teeth.

Claire felt her own mouth move as the woman spoke. Her lips moved in the shapes of the words; strange, unthought-of words urging themselves up from her stomach, into her dry mouth – she felt the wind of them pass over her lips, yet she was not speaking! Somehow, the woman in the mirror was *using* her.

'You *had* to do it!' the woman screamed delightedly. 'You had to try the dress on, didn't you? I knew you would. I knew that some day, someone would try the dress on. Some day the trunk would be opened and the dress would be found. It is a very pretty dress.'

Claire wanted to scream, to run away as fast as her legs would take her, but her legs were no longer her own to use. Her mouth was no longer her own to scream with – her tongue was not her own.

'Soon I shall have you!' cried the old woman. 'Soon I shall have a body again. A young body, filled with life and movement, with years of life ahead!' The voice was now a banshee wail of ecstasy. Frantically, Claire tried to rip the dress away from herself, but as she raised her arms she felt something pulling her back. Her arms would not respond.

'Don't fight me, little girl!'

Concentrating hard, Claire willed herself to control her own movements. But she could not. Her head would not turn away from the horrible image in the mirror.

Her legs would not move.

'You can't fight me!' the old woman crackled.

The dress, Claire thought. I must get it off. No sooner had the thoughts formed in her mind, than another thought occurred to her. You can't get the dress off. It is impossible. You will never get the dress off.

Now the old woman was grunting, moving herself in the mirror image, causing Claire to move as if she were nothing more than a simple puppet on a string.

Claire felt her arms jerk.

She felt her head move this way and that way as the old woman tested out her body as if it were nothing more than a new pair of shoes to get used to.

'I'm nearly there!' the woman shrieked.

'No!' Claire shouted. Hearing her own voice seemed to give her strength. If only she could will her hands to tear the dress away.

'Just a minute or two!'

Claire could feel her strength ebbing rapidly.

'Almost . . . there!'

One last try, thought Claire.

One last try.

It was no use. Claire struggled as hard as she was able, using all the muscles in her body to make her fingers grip the dress. But the woman's will was stronger than her own, and Claire felt her fingers being forced back, unlocked one by one until she was exhausted with the unequal struggle.

Even the thoughts in her head were not her own. One part of her brain kept insisting that she had to run, another was smoothly coaxing her to stay. She was split into two people – both fighting for control of her body. Tears ran in rivulets down her face as her mouth twisted into the characteristic, evil grin of the old woman. One second she was thinking as Claire would think – next she was the old woman, biting, scratching and clawing to gain control.

'Look at me!' the old woman screamed from the mirror. Claire felt her head being forced around so that she had to look at the old woman, the muscles of her neck straining in an effort to turn away.

'I must control you,' said the voice in her head.

'You won't . . . you won't.'

'Give up! You can't hold out much longer. You are only a child.'

She felt her legs move stiffly, so that she stood squarely before the mirror, and she felt her arms rise as if they no longer belonged to her. She saw the angular, bony fingers pat the grey hair into place and felt the exultation of the old woman surging through her body.

'It's good to have a body again,' she heard herself say. 'Now I can claim what is rightfully mine. Oh, how long I have waited for this very day.'

The mixture of enjoyment and revulsion curdled in Claire's stomach as she watched the image preen itself in the mirror. Her own thoughts were gradually being blotted out by this woman's thoughts, her body was gradually becoming the property of this woman.

In her mind she could see Talgar Castle – as if from a great distance; she could feel herself experiencing the old woman's greed. One day, she thought, all this will be mine. One day, when my father is dead, I will own Talgar!

And Claire saw Talgar in her mind's eye, exactly as it was a hundred years ago. She saw the great hall and the shiny staircase and the servants bustling about their tasks. These thoughts were in Claire's mind – but they were not Claire's own thoughts.

Then she found herself standing by a bed, looking at the waxen face of a bearded man. He was trying to speak to her. 'Everything I have – is for – Paul.'

Claire felt the old woman's rage surging through her body and her mouth opened involuntarily. She heard the words gush out in a torrent.

'Father! How can you do this to me? You know I have always loved Talgar. Why leave it all to Paul?'

90

'He is my eldest son,' came the reply from the man in the bed.

'A spendthrift!' Claire found herself shouting. 'Do I have to wait until his death to inherit Talgar?'

As she enacted the memories of events which had taken place a hundred years ago, Claire became fascinated, feeling a sense of cruel injustice that the father should have treated his daughter so. She knew, as well as the old woman knew, that Paul would only sell Talgar to live a life of ease on the profits. He did not care for the castle.

Now Claire was torn between running away and surrendering her thoughts to the old woman. She knew that Paul had returned to claim his inheritance, but only after a great number of years. The old woman had kept Talgar in good condition for him, thinking that he would never, ever return. But he did.

Paul was old and his hands were gnarled and trembling as he went up the stairs on his first night back at Talgar. Claire could see it all quite clearly. She could feel the old woman's impotent rage against her brother. She could experience the evil thoughts.

Then a terrifying image came into her head. She was standing at the top of the staircase, hands extended, pushing the old man back. 'You shall never have Talgar!' she was shouting. 'Never! Never!'

Paul fell back down the stairs . . . down . . . down . . . down.

Already she could feel the jubilant expression on the old woman's face. 'I shall keep Talgar!' she was crying. Then Claire felt herself slipping, watching the bannister rails spinning by. The old woman must have fallen too! She could only have inherited Talgar for a few seconds before plunging to her own death.

Now the woman was staring at her soberly, her

face expressionless, her eyes misted over with the dreadful memories of her shameful deed. Seizing the advantage, Claire opened her mouth to call for help. At the same time she started to run. Run! She willed her leaden body to move forward, each movement draining vital energy from her. The old woman was alert now, watching from the mirror, feeling and knowing everything which Claire was experiencing.

'You can't escape!' she shouted.

The voice was inside her and outside and all around her; the laughter echoed in her head. Too late. Too late now. The effort had drained her of all resistance. She fell to the floor, sobbing inside, unable even to make tears come to her own eyes. It was defeat. She could see through her eyes, yet she could not control them. Her body had feeling, yet it was not hers to use. Now there was nothing left to fight with. The old woman had won.

Vaguely, as in a dream, she saw a man standing over her. She saw concern upon his face as he bent low. A woman was standing in the background, her horror-stricken eyes watching as the man struggled to tear the dress away.

'It's choking her!' the man cried. 'Help me get the dress off.'

Suddenly the woman sprang into action. She knelt next to the man, pulling away the dress with her hands, tearing at the flounces, snapping the ribbons as if they were made of paper.

As the dress came away, Claire could hear unbearable cries of anguish in her head; her body flooded with fear.

Away with the ribbons! Away with the flounces! An ear-piercing cry filled the air as the dress finally came away.

'Hello, Mr Holly,' Claire said as she recognized the man's face.

'Don't talk,' he said. 'That silly dress nearly strangled you. You looked awful.' He lifted her gently, took her downstairs into the warm kitchen and left her with Mrs Holly. When he returned to the kitchen he was carrying the shreds of the old dress and the oil painting.

'What are you going to do?' Mrs Holly asked in surprise.

He did not answer her. Taking the dress, he rolled it into a bundle and thrust it into the fire; then he tore the canvas portrait from its frame, held down the frame beneath his foot and snapped it like matchwood.

As the dress and the portrait were consumed by the hungry, licking flames, terrible screams of agony filled Talgar Castle, causing Janet to run in from the garden, wide-eyed and fearful. And when the last shreds had burned away, turned black and died, there was peace.

PAGET
Lucy Norris

Have you ever had something happen to you that
was so strange, so weird and unexplainable, that it
gave you goose-pimples every time you thought
about it?

I have. It all happened last summer but I still get
a strange feeling whenever I think about it. My
brothers were there at the time but they weren't quite
so involved as I was. I'm the only one who knows
what it feels like to be a ghost. At least, I *think* I
do. Even now I'm not absolutely sure what really
happened to me that night.

My name is Cora, by the way, and I am eleven
years old. My brother David is thirteen and Jimmie
is eight. The summer this all happened my mother
had been very ill, and my father had taken us all to
stay with Auntie Jean and Uncle Harry. They lived
in a very large old house right in the country, surrounded by acres of farmland. Mother was still very
frail and spent most of the day resting. Dad, when he
wasn't playing golf, went around with Uncle Harry
looking at the animals and visiting other farms. Dad
said Uncle was a gentleman farmer – whatever that
may mean. Auntie Jean was always too busy in the
kitchen to bother about us, so we children were left
in peace to do pretty much as we wanted.

The weather had been gloriously sunny and warm
most of the time but one morning, towards the end
of the first week, it turned heavy and overcast. Before

we had finished breakfast, the first raindrops were splashing against the window panes.

'Now we shall have to play indoors,' growled David.

Dad peered over the top of his newspaper. 'Just make sure you play quietly, then,' he said, looking at each of us in turn. 'I don't want your mother to be disturbed.'

Auntie Jean offered us a pack of 'Happy Families' but as one of the cards was missing it rather spoilt the game. We then spent an hour playing 'Consequences', until Jimmie broke the point on his pencil, and we didn't have a sharpener. We wandered down to the kitchen to ask Auntie Jean if she had another pencil, but she seemed to be in a bad mood over something for she sent us packing when we had barely set foot in the door.

'Now what are we going to do?' grumbled David, throwing himself untidily into an armchair.

'Yes. Now what are we going to do?' echoed Jimmie, also dropping into a chair and scowling just like David. Jimmie is always copying everything David does.

'I know,' I said brightly. 'Let's each tell a ghost story and see who can make up the most scary one.'

'Sounds a silly idea to me,' said David bluntly.

'Sounds a silly idea to me too,' said Jimmie.

'Suggest something better then,' I challenged.

They thought deeply for several minutes but, as neither could think of anything at all, they reluctantly agreed to my idea.

We did Eeny Meeny Miny Mo to see who should go first; I won.

Although it was only midday, the room had grown quite dark and we could hear the occasional distant rumble of thunder. Not that we were afraid of thunder-storms, we weren't, but it did help to give a suitable atmosphere for telling a ghost story.

'It happened on a dark and stormy night,' I began. 'A night when all wise people stayed safely in their homes. It was the night when the headless phantom was known to walk the wind-swept moors crying out in vain for mercy and forgiveness . . .'

'Huh!' snorted David derisively. 'How could he cry out if he was headless?'

'Yes, how could he?' queried Jimmie.

I pretended not to hear their remarks. I've had this trouble with them before and have learnt not to stop and argue, as that always spoils the atmosphere of the story. Instead I did some fast thinking and rectified my mistake as I continued:

'This was the most frightening thing about the phantom, because those who had seen him swore he was headless, yet his voice could be heard loud and clear. Where, everybody asked in fear, did that voice come from?'

I took a sly peek at the boys and noted with considerable satisfaction that the smirks had left their faces. Jimmie, in fact, was looking quite saucer-eyed. This was better than I had hoped for. Even David stared across the room in silence.

'The headless phantom went up to the lonely cottage. His hairy, black, claw-like hand reached out towards the door and . . .'

Jimmie gave a stifled cry and cringed back into the armchair, his eyes popping with fear.

I tried not to show how delighted I was with the success of my story. 'Don't be silly, Jimmie,' I said sternly. 'It's only make-believe.'

Jimmie didn't seem to hear me. He was staring straight past me at something behind my back. I heard a rustling movement and turned to look. A hairy, black, claw-like hand was creeping slowly round the half-open door. One quick glance was enough for me; I let out an ear-piercing shriek and vaulted over the back of the settee.

'My sainted aunt! What's going on in here?' demanded Uncle Harry's gardener, as he shuffled into the room carrying a large potted plant in his arms.

David was the first to find his voice. 'We thought you were a ghost,' he explained.

'A ghost, did you say?' chuckled Elliot as he carefully placed the plant on a windowsill. 'No. That's one thing I'm not. Someone been telling you about our ghosts, then, have they?'

We looked at each other in surprise. 'Ghosts?' we chorused. 'What ghosts?'

Elliot peered at us over his gold-rimmed spectacles. 'Why, the ghosts that haunt this old house, of course. Leastways, they don't haunt this part of the house. Only the east wing or, rather, the ruins of the east wing. That part was never rebuilt after the fire. Completely gutted it was.'

'Tell us about the ghosts,' we begged as he turned to leave the room.

'Well now,' he began, taking a piece of rag from the pocket of his oilskin and wiping his grimy hands. 'There isn't much to tell, really. It happened about a hundred years ago. Sir Robert and Lady Lee were living here at the time. They had one child; a little boy. One evening the child disappeared and the parents searched frantically for him all over the house but he was nowhere to be found. Then, while the whole household was still looking and calling for him, a fire started in the east wing where the nursery was. It is said that one of the servants must have knocked over a lamp and that started the fire.

Anyway, there was a stiff breeze blowing that night and in no time at all the whole of that wing was ablaze.'

'That must have been a frightening sight,' said David.

Elliot nodded. 'Sir Robert ordered everyone to leave the building, but her ladyship, believing her little boy might still be in that part of the house, ran back into the burning nursery. Sir Robert followed in an attempt to rescue her before the building collapsed but he was too late to save her or himself. They perished together in the blazing inferno.'

'What happened to the little boy?' I asked.

Elliot shrugged his shoulders. 'That's the puzzling thing. They found the bodies of Sir Robert and his wife but, although a thorough search was made amongst the wreckage, the child's body was never found. It's my belief he was stolen by gipsies. There were plenty of them passing through here in those days. Anyway, nothing was ever heard of him again. Next time you go by the church, have a look at the tomb under the old yew tree. That's where Sir Robert and his wife were buried. On the side panel it mentions the little boy and how he disappeared without trace.'

'I suppose Sir Robert and his wife still haunt this house looking for their little son,' said David.

Elliot nodded. 'That's about the size of it. And I guess they are doomed to do so for eternity. He isn't likely to turn up now.'

'Have you seen their ghosts?' asked David. 'Please tell us if you have. We really are most interested.'

'Well now,' smiled Elliot. 'Yes, I've seen them. Many times.'

'What happens?' asked Jimmie.

'Nothing much,' replied Elliot. 'Around nine

98

o'clock in the evening – about the time that the fire started – two shadowy figures move about the ruins of the east wing. If you try to go too close, they disappear. Leastways, that's how it has always been with me. So now I just watch from my cottage window.'

'And do they come and search every night?' I asked.

'Oh, dear no,' said Elliot. 'Only on the anniversary of the little boy's disappearance.'

'The night of the fire, in fact?' said David.

Elliot nodded.

'When is the anniversary?' I asked.

'When is it?' repeated Elliot. 'Ah, that'd be telling.' And before any of us could stop him he had shuffled from the room.

Of course we ran after him but he was out through the front door before we could catch him and, as it was raining and we didn't have our coats handy, we had to let him go.

During lunchtime David asked Uncle Harry about the fire.

'That was before my time, David,' he laughed.

'Yes, but do you know the date that it happened?' asked David, trying to appear unconcerned.

'Sorry, old chap. Haven't the foggiest,' replied Uncle. 'Why do you ask? Elliot hasn't been filling your heads with all that stupid nonsense of his about ghosts, has he?'

'Ghosts, Uncle?' we chorused innocently, as though we had never heard of such things before. (Well, we could hardly let Elliot down, now could we?)

'I just wondered,' shrugged Uncle Harry and promptly changed the subject.

When we had finished lunch, David beckoned

excitedly to us and hurried from the room. We found him waiting in the hall.

'I've thought of a way to find out the date of the fire,' he whispered. 'All we have to do is go to the churchyard and find Sir Robert's tomb. The date will be on there. Come on, it stopped raining ten minutes ago.'

We had no difficulty in finding the tomb. It was a large and imposing-looking one. Eagerly we read the inscription and found what we were looking for:

'Departed from this life on the third day of September in the year of Our Lord 1871.'

We stared at each other in blank amazement. David repeated the date out loud.

'A hundred years ago today,' I gasped. A strange little thrill ran up and down my spine. 'That means . . .'

'That the ghosts will walk tonight,' exclaimed David.

'Ooh, er!' Jimmie said nervously. Then, seeing the look on our faces, he added hastily: 'That should be fun.'

'No wonder Elliot wouldn't tell us. He guessed we would want to watch,' I said.

'You bet we're going to watch,' declared David.

'Oh, er,' muttered Jimmie again.

'You don't have to watch if you don't want to,' we told him. But we knew that, no matter how scared Jimmie might feel, he wouldn't be left out of anything.

We discussed our plan on the way home. The grown-ups would be in the lounge playing bridge all evening, so there was no fear of our being disturbed. If we hid in the little summer house on the far side of the lawn, we should have an uninterrupted view of the east wing.

We were very excited and Jimmie made matters worse by getting into one of his silly moods. He would keep tweaking my hair and saying he hadn't touched me, that it must have been a ghost. By the time we went into supper I was feeling quite annoyed with him. So that when he deliberately jogged my elbow and made me spill my glass of milk, I was so angry I hit him.

Uncle Harry just smiled and said something about little birds in their nest agreeing, but Dad was furious. He was developing a cold and that always makes him irritable.

'Go to your room and remain there for the rest of the evening,' he told me.

'But, there's something special I must do tonight,' I pleaded. 'Please don't send me to bed.'

To give Jimmie his due, he did speak up on my behalf. But Dad was adamant. I thought my heart would break with disappointment as I went up to my bedroom.

I looked at the little clock on the mantelpiece. It said eight-thirty. From the window, in the dusk, I could see the summer house, but it was not possible to see the east wing; not even when I tried leaning out as far as I dared. I heard footsteps below and dodged back but it was only the shadowy shapes of David and Jimmie going across to the summer house to hide and watch.

They looked up at me and waved sympathetically, then hid themselves behind some deckchairs. I watched and waited, and again peered at the clock. In the failing light I could just make out that it was approaching nine o'clock. As far as I knew this might be the only time in my entire life when I would have the chance to see a ghost . . . two ghosts, in fact! I had never disobeyed my parents before but I felt desperate . . .

I opened my door. There was no one in the corridor and I could reach the back staircase unseen. I tiptoed down the stairs and through the kitchen, and let myself out of the back door. I could not join David and Jimmie in the summer house because that meant crossing the lawn and Dad might see me. My only hope was to wend my way through the rhododendron bushes and hide in the boathouse beside the lake. It was rather a long way from the house but any view was better than none.

I was crouched just inside the half-open door of the boathouse, my eyes fixed on the distant ruins of the east wing, when I heard a movement behind me. I could barely see the small boy huddled in the dim far corner of the boathouse. His face was thin and pale, and he was shivering in the damp night air.

'Who are you?' I asked in surprise.

He didn't answer but shrank further back into the shadows and began to weep softly.

I crawled nearer to him. 'Don't cry,' I said. 'I'm not going to hurt you. What are you doing here, anyway?'

'I've run away,' he sobbed. 'Papa sent me to bed because I was rude to my tutor. So I ran away and came here to hide. Now I cannot go home.'

'Why can't you go home? Are you lost?'

He shook his head. 'No, I'm not lost. I live in that house there.' He pointed through the doorway towards my uncle's house and I felt my blood run cold. Instinctively I pulled away from him.

'You're Sir Robert's little boy, aren't you?' I whispered.

He nodded. 'Yes. I'm Paget.'

'Do you know how long you have been hiding?' I asked.

He nodded again. 'A long time.'

'Why didn't you go home when your mother was calling for you?'

He began to weep again. 'I started to but I slipped and fell in the lake. I couldn't swim and the water kept pulling me under. It was dark and very cold.'

I looked at the oily stillness of the lake and shivered. Somewhere, under that water . . .

'Then you know that you are dead?' I asked nervously.

He nodded. 'Yes. I do now but I didn't at first. I wondered why people looked at me but never spoke to me. Do you think that Mama and Papa know?'

I explained as gently as I could how his parents had perished in the fire. 'They are sleeping peacefully in the churchyard,' I concluded.

Then I remembered why I was hiding in the boathouse. 'No, they are not!' I cried. 'They are still looking for you. They have never stopped looking for you. And tonight they will return again to look for you. All you have to do is to go to them.'

I ran outside. It was growing quite dark. I could see lights in the downstairs rooms of the house. In the ruins of the east wing I thought I saw two figures moving.

'Come on, Paget,' I implored. 'You must hurry or you will miss them. Please hurry. It must be nearly time.'

Paget was standing by the edge of the lake. 'I can't,' he cried. 'I can't move. The water is too strong. It won't let me go. I can't fight it.'

'You can! You can!' I screamed. 'Let me help you. Take hold of my hand.'

He reached out and took my hand in his. It felt

cold and wet. I tried to pull him towards me and suddenly I was very frightened. Something was pulling both of us towards the lake. I tried to back away but I couldn't move. I held on tightly to Paget. 'Keep close to me,' I yelled. Paget seemed to grow bigger and bigger. He appeared to flow over me like a heavy wet blanket and I felt I was sinking down into inky black depths. I couldn't breathe. I tried to call out but only a gurgling sound came from my throat. I couldn't see Paget any more but I felt he was all round me and, in some way, had even become part of me. My lungs felt as though they would burst and my legs were so heavy they dragged me down, down, down. And I knew I was fighting for my life.

I think I was on the point of losing consciousness when I remembered Paget saying he couldn't swim. But I *could* swim. My father had taught us to swim almost before we could walk. I needn't drown, as Paget had done, because I knew how to swim. I struck out and fought against the wet blackness . . .

And suddenly I could hear Mama calling: 'Paget. Paget, where are you?'

'I'm here, Mama, I'm here!' I shouted. And the blackness fell away. I found I was running towards the house. My legs felt weak but I didn't stop. I could see the flames shooting out of the roof and Mama standing at the nursery window calling to me. She saw me and held out her arms. 'Mama, Mama,' I cried, and ran into the flames and into the safety of her arms.

Ever since, I have tried to remember exactly what did happen to me that night when I ran into the east wing, but my mind is a blank. A complete blank except for one thing: a recollection of relief and of supreme happiness.

David and Jimmie told me afterwards that they were watching from the summer house but they didn't see any flames and they didn't see Lady Lee. However, they did see a small boy, dressed in old-fashioned clothes, running towards the house from the direction of the lake. They watched him run into the ruins of the east wing and disappear suddenly. Then they saw Elliot hurrying towards the ruins and saw him bend down and lift something in his arms. They came out of hiding and ran across to help.

I opened my eyes to find I was being carried into the house in Elliot's arms, while every now and again I caught a glimpse of either David's or Jimmie's chalk-white face peering anxiously at me.

You can imagine the fuss the grown-ups made when they saw the state I was in: exhausted, soaking wet and covered in green slime. I was given a bath and put to bed. The next morning my parents demanded an explanation. But they refused to believe me when I told them the truth. In fact, they laughed.

Elliot didn't laugh, though. He said he knew something special had happened that night when he saw Sir Robert and Lady Lee walk away from the house leading a small boy by the hand.

LET'S PLAY GHOSTS!
Pamela Vincent

'You're talking absolute rot,' said Perry.

'I don't care whether you believe it or not,' shrugged Hugh.

'But we've lived here for years. We'd know if the place were haunted.'

'Not unless you're the sort of people who *feel* these things.'

Perry laughed. 'Oh, feeling! It's easy enough to say you *feel* things, but when have you ever *seen* a ghost?'

'I believe you, Hugh,' said Charlotte, Perry's young sister, when Hugh didn't answer.

'You would,' said her brother, scornfully. '*You* won't even pass a churchyard when it's dark.'

'You don't want to worry about that, Charlie,' Hugh smiled. 'The ones buried in churchyards are all right, they don't need to haunt.'

'But it's creepy with all those funny tombstones,' shivered the little girl.

'It's much creepier in your dining-room,' said Hugh.

'What's creepy about the dining-room?'

They all jumped as Mr Baxter came in and started vaguely looking for something.

'Hugh says it's haunted, Daddy,' replied Charlotte, her eyes shining with excitement.

'Um? Well, suicides often do haunt, don't they?'

106

With relief, Mr Baxter found his tobacco pouch under a cushion, and started to wander away, but–

'What!' exclaimed both his children.

'What are you talking about, Dad?' demanded Perry.

Mr Baxter looked surprised.

'I thought you knew, You were a bit young when we first came here, but I'm sure something was said about someone committing suicide in the house.'

'*Hugh* said it was a n'orrible murder,' said Perry.

'It seemed like that to me,' said Hugh, puzzled.

'No, I'm sure it was suicide,' Mr Baxter frowned, searching his memory.

'Gosh, I thought houses had to be hundreds of years old to have ghosts,' said Charlotte, looking around their cheerful, modern room.

'This was sixty-odd years ago,' grunted her father round the pipe he was now lighting with too many matches. 'Before even your old Dad was born.'

'How did he do it?' asked Perry, with gruesome interest.

'It was a girl,' said Hugh. 'A young girl.'

'That's right,' agreed Mr Baxter. 'She took poison, I think. Don't know why – blighted in love, I expect.'

'No, she was too young for that,' said Hugh.

'Never too young,' said Mr Baxter briskly. 'Look at Charlie here, always in love with someone or other.'

'I'm not!' cried Charlotte.

'You are,' retorted Perry, 'there's that spotty boy in the choir –'

'He's no spottier than you –'

'Shut up, kids,' said Mr Baxter, 'I want to talk about Hugh's being psychic –'

'Please, Mr Baxter, I'd rather forget it. I wouldn't

107

have mentioned it, but I felt so bad in the dining-room that the others noticed.'

'But it's so int'resting, Hugh,' said Charlie. 'I wish *I* were psytic.'

Hugh shook his head.

'No, Charlie, it's very uncomfortable.'

'It creates rather a problem,' observed Mr Baxter, thoughtfully. 'We can't have you starving to death while you're staying with us, but you say going into the dining-room upsets you.'

'That's all right, we'll eat in the kitchen,' decided Charlie. 'I'll tell Mummy.'

'She won't like that,' said Perry, 'we always use the dining-room for guests.'

'Hugh'd rather be one of the family – wouldn't you?' smiled Mr Baxter.

'If it's not putting Mrs Baxter to any trouble.'

'It saves bother,' said Charlotte, 'but don't tell your parents we made you eat in the kitchen, will you?'

The holiday was crowded enough for them to forget about the ghost. Hugh's parents were in South America so the two schoolfriends had all summer to spend together, sometimes letting Charlie tag along, sometimes joining up with Baxter cousins of about their own age, Colin and Sue. A fortnight was spent at the seaside – and then they came home to bad weather, with nothing to do but mope indoors.

'D'you know we've got a ghost?' said Perry, bored with sprawling on the floor losing at Monopoly.

Hugh flashed him an annoyed glance and Charlotte exclaimed:

'Oh, Perry, you weren't supposed to say!'

'Why not?' cried Sue. 'We're cousins, we've a right to know.'

'Yes, you must tell us,' said Colin eagerly. Even winning, he'd had enough Monopoly.

'Hugh, you tell them.'

'Hugh? So *he* was allowed to hear about it,' said Sue indignantly.

'*He* told *us* – oh, Hugh, stop frowning at me like that,' said Perry. 'You might be a sport and let them in on it.'

'Nothing to tell, really, is there? Your father said a young girl took poison about sixty years ago, that's all.'

'It isn't all – what about the ghost?' asked Sue.

'That's why we haven't been eating in the dining-room lately,' said Charlotte helpfully.

'You mean it's in there?' said Colin. 'Why has it only just started haunting, then?'

Perry and Charlotte looked at Hugh, and after a pause he said:

'I'm the only one to feel her presence.'

'What does she look like?' asked Sue.

'I don't know, I can't see her.'

'Then how d'you know she's there?'

'You wouldn't understand unless you felt it too.'

'But why you?' asked Colin. 'You'd think a ghost would be more interested in the people who live in the house.'

'She can't get through to them,' explained Hugh. 'You have to be sort of tuned-in on the right wave-length. Can't we talk about something else?'

'Don't be mean, Hugh,' said Charlotte, gently. 'We're all fascinated.'

'What's she like – what's her name?' Sue was still asking questions.

'I didn't hold a conversation with her. It was as if the thought flashed into my mind: there's a young girl here, someone's poisoned her, it's horrible – and I couldn't stay in the room with it.'

'You said it again, that she was murdered,' Perry noticed. 'Dad said it was suicide.'

'It might have been an accident, but I don't think she *wanted* to die –' began Hugh.

'That's why she's haunting,' interrupted Sue. 'Hugh, you might be able to help her.'

They all looked at Hugh expectantly.

'I don't see how.'

'Go and ask her,' said Sue.

'You don't know what it's like,' protested Hugh. 'It's like fighting your way through a – through a cloud, something you can't get away from.'

'You're scared,' said Colin.

Hugh fidgeted.

'I think it's mean not to try to help her,' said Sue.

Perry suddenly marched across to the dining-room and flung open the door.

'Come on, ghostie, rattle your chains for us!' he called. 'Give us a fright, too, like poor old Hugh!'

Hugh leapt to his feet.

'All right, I'll try.'

He paused with his hand on the door.

'I'll come with you,' offered Charlie uncertainly.

Hugh shook his head, smiling at the little girl.

'It wouldn't work, Charlie – she wouldn't talk to me then.'

He went inside quickly, closing the door behind him. The others crowded nearer.

'I can't hear what they're saying,' complained Charlotte.

'Hugh's talking, but I can't hear anyone else,' said Sue.

'Of course not,' said Perry, 'you don't believe there really is a ghost, do you?'

They strained their ears.

The door opened suddenly and Hugh came out, his face pale. The room beyond looked very dark.

'She's lonely, poor child,' said Hugh. His voice dropped to a horrified whisper. 'She wanted me to stay with her!'

'Come and sit down, Hugh, you look awful,' said Sue.

'I feel awful.'

He sank into a chair and closed his eyes.

'She's drained me of all my energy –'

'We couldn't hear anyone except you,' said Perry flatly.

'No, she was very faint.'

'What did she say?' asked Charlotte.

'That she'd been alone with old people when she was alive, and now she's got nobody.' Hugh's eyes opened, revealing horror as he went on, 'I didn't think she'd let me go!'

'How could she stop you?' asked Colin.

'I don't know, it was like fighting my way out of something clammy and clinging that I couldn't see, and all the time she was begging me not to leave her –'

'Did you find out more about the murder?' asked Perry, practically.

'She said her aunt did it. Her aunt by marriage – the uncle was Lavender's guardian – that's her name, Lavender – and he inherited all her parents' money when she died.'

'How sordid,' said sue. 'I hope they came to a sticky end, too!'

'It wasn't the uncle's fault. But you're right, the wicked aunt died after a long and painful illness – only it didn't do Lavender any good because she never confessed to the murder and people still thought Lavender had committed suicide.'

'No wonder she's haunting,' said Sue. 'How stupid of everybody, as if a child would take poison on purpose!'

'The aunt made out Lavender had always been a bit strange in the head, and she even had a piece of paper Lavender had scribbled on one day when she was extra unhappy. It said: "I hate my life, why don't I die?" '

'Isn't it sad,' quavered Charlotte, her eyes filling with tears. 'I feel so sorry for her.'

'Yes, she needs friends,' said Sue. 'What can we do?'

'Priests used to exorcize ghosts, d'you think they still can?' suggested Colin.

'How do we prove we've got a ghost?' asked Perry. 'We've only got Hugh's word for it.'

'We'll get Daddy to talk to the priest,' said Charlie.

Perry looked at her.

'Poor old Dad, everyone in the neighbourhood thinks he's dotty as it is.'

'Perry, how can you say such an awful thing about your own father?' squeaked Charlie.

'You must admit he's an absent-minded professor type, not exactly in the same world with the rest of us,' Perry pointed out.

The dining-room door closed with a click and they all stared at it.

'I didn't think there was any wind,' said Colin.

'There isn't,' said Perry. 'That's why it's getting so dark, all the clouds are overhead.'

'Where's Sue?' asked Hugh.

Perry glanced at the dining-room door.

'Gone ghost-hunting?' he said.

'But she mustn't!' cried Hugh. 'Perry, get her out of there.'

'Get her yourself,' retorted Perry.

'You two! Who'd imagine you were friends?' declared Colin, flinging the door open. 'Oh! She's not here.'

'Well, we didn't see her go in –' began Perry.

'She *is* in there,' said Hugh, quietly.

'Don't be daft,' said Perry, 'there's nowhere for a mouse to hide.'

He went in and opened the sideboard cupboards, to show their crammed interiors.

'I don't mean she's hiding,' said Hugh, oddly.

Colin stared at him, then understood.

'Come off it, Hugh – Sue's a solid, living human being.'

'Not any more.'

'Oo, it's cold,' shivered Charlie.

The room was *cold*. Very cold. And quite dark now, rain beating against the windows.

'She's somewhere in the house, we'll find her,' said Perry briskly.

But they didn't. They searched everywhere.

'Come on, Sue, you win!' called Colin.

'The joke's gone on long enough,' added Perry.

There was no answer. The only sound was a clock ticking away the time Sue had been missing, and the rain dripping from every ledge outside.

'It's not funny any more,' shouted Perry.

They went back to the sitting-room, which seemed empty in the electric light's glare.

'I think,' said Charlotte, in a small voice. 'Lavender's got a friend now.'

'I'm afraid so, Charlie,' agreed Hugh, sadly.

The little girl burst into tears.

'When are Daddy and Mummy coming home?' she wailed.

'Not till late,' answered Perry.

'Can't we reach them on the telephone?' asked Colin.

'No. anyway, what could we say? What could *they* do?'

They sank into gloomy silence.

'We didn't tap the walls for secret panels,' said Colin suddenly.

'What have you been reading lately?' scoffed Perry. 'You don't have secret panels in houses like this.'

'It's worth trying.'

'It's no use, Colin,' said Hugh, miserably. 'You know what's happened to Sue.'

'I *don't*,' returned Colin. 'She might have fallen through somewhere and be lying unconscious.'

'There's no room for secret compartments,' insisted Perry.

'*You* didn't know that there was a ghost here,' said Colin reasonably. 'It's worth trying.'

'Well, she's your sister,' shrugged Perry.

They heard Colin thumping the walls, shifting furniture.

And then the door closed with a soft, but firm, click.

Hugh leapt to his feet and raced to open it, then turned to the others, his face stricken.

'She's getting stronger,' he said. 'Lavender's absorbing their energy –'

Colin had gone.

'Those cousins of mine are always up to something,' Perry tried to speak confidently.

He strode over to the window and leaned out.

'Can't see any footprints –'

'But it's raining,' cried Charlie. 'They wouldn't go out there – oh, I'm so frightened.'

Hugh took her hand.

'We'll all stay together, and it'll be all right – Perry, come away from there –'

'Why, do you think I'm going to disappear in front of your very eyes?'

Perry was cross now that he was beginning to feel frightened, too.

'You might.'

Perry shook his wet hair and banged the window shut – and at that moment a door slammed upstairs.

The boys looked at each other, then raced for the stairs.

'Wait for me!' screamed Charlie, fumbling with a loose slipper, but they didn't stop to listen.

'Don't worry about them, Charlie,' Sue spoke from the darkness of the dining-room.

'Sue!'

'Sh! Don't give us away – you come and hide, too.'

'I *knew* you must be somewhere!' cried Charlotte, joyfully, running to join her cousins.

'There's no one up here,' yelled Perry. 'We've looked all over.'

He and Hugh bounded three steps at a time down to the gloomy hall.

'Charlie? Where've *you* got to now?'

'Oh no, not little Charlie,' groaned Hugh.

'Charlotte, don't fool around,' said Perry, sharply. Silence.

'She wouldn't be able to keep it up,' said Perry, doubtfully. 'She'd laugh and give the game away–'

He looked at his friend with stricken eyes.

'I'm sorry, Perry,' said Hugh, gently.

'How can we get her back?' asked Perry.

'There's no way back.'

'But – we can't leave her there, wherever she is. She'll be so frightened without me –'

115

His voice trailed off.

'She likes me,' said Hugh, 'I'll go and look after her.'

'Where?'

Hugh looked towards the dining-room, its door invitingly half-open.

'You can't, Hugh. You said you wouldn't be able to come back.'

'No,' agreed his friend, walking away.

'You mustn't,' cried Perry urgently.

Hugh smiled and went into the darkness. The door closed behind him, looking as if it would never open again.

Perry sank into a chair and looked at his own thoughts, while the house grew colder – and quieter.

'It's all rubbish,' he told himself. 'If Hugh hadn't said anything, we'd have gone on using the dining-room and nothing would have happened. He started it all . . . But *where* have they all disappeared to?'

Slowly Perry became aware that the house was not so quiet as it had been. There were odd shufflings and clicking noises. And wasn't that Charlie's giggle?

He looked towards the dining-room. A line of light showed under the door.

With one bound he had reached it and flung the door open with a crash.

Startled faces turned in his direction.

'Perry! We thought you were never coming!' shrieked Charlotte, running from her seat at the long table to fling her arms around his neck.

'We wondered how long you'd sit there by yourself,' grinned Colin.

'This game's almost over,' said Sue, shaking the dice, 'then you can join in.'

Perry was almost speechless with a mixture of relief and rage.

'You rotten lot! Enjoying yourselves while I've been going dotty in there! I never want to see any of you again!'

He turned to go.

'You haven't been introduced to Lavender yet,' said Hugh.

Perry followed his glance and for the first time noticed a newcomer, a girl not much older than Charlotte, with long, golden hair tied back with a ribbon, and an old-fashioned dress. And blue eyes shining from a face flushed with happiness.

'Now we're all here,' said Lavender breathlessly, 'we can have fun for ever and ever, can't we?'

RUN FOR YOUR LIFE
Philip Sidney Jennings

'Take your marks!'

This was the moment I dreaded, a hundred and twenty boys shuffling their feet behind the creosoted starting line, the numbing December wind, the blurred, staring faces of parents, friends and officials, the mad dash across the school field before we hit the hill and the pain began. I was shaking with cold and nerves. A few minutes ago we'd been laughing and joking in the warm changing rooms and listening to Mr Relph's route instructions.

'Little bit longer this year, lads. You go up the hill, across Bog's Field, through the wood, but then you come out of it and go through Toll's Tunnel. This brings you out into the crescent field, which with any luck will bring you back to where you started. Once round the cinder track, of course. Any questions?'

'Is it the first three that go forward to the Counties?'

That was red-haired Spinak's question. I didn't know why he asked it. He was a natural. He'd never lost a race. Mr Relph nodded. 'The first there. The third would probably be a reserve.'

'Bit dark and boggy, that Toll's Tunnel,' Quinn said. He was a tall, stooping figure with a built-in chuckle and legs that never gave up. He always ran second to Spinak.

'Get set!'

The long line of boys crouched a little further forward.

Before we'd left the changing room Mr Relph had had a word with me. 'Danny, you've been in the first ten for some time, you've trained hard – see what you can pull out.'

That was the frustrating thing. I'd always been a good cross-country runner but never quite good enough to get a county place, which was my dream.

Crack! The sound of the starter's pistol released us.

The charge across the school field was always mad and full of bravado. Everybody was watching and cheering. We always ran this part like it was a print. When we hit the hill the moment of truth arrived. Some boys went up it bent forward, gasping, their hands on their knees.

I got a good start, and half way up the hill I could make out the red-haired Spinak gaining the top, tall Quinn not far behind, then a knot of five or six running together. My inner voice started up as it always does on these long cold runs. 'Watch your breathing. Keep it up. Bit faster. Get your rhythm. Spinak's going too far ahead. Don't lose him.' But I always did. Or he lost me. He'd been under–14s champion, under–15s, and now looked like he was well on the way to taking the under–16s.

'Do you want a county place or not?'

There it was, that inner voice, always exhorting, questioning, urging me on.

The sky was a mass of heavy grey and white clouds. The wind was brutal. My eyes smarted and misted with water. I felt the old agony of being in the first ten runners. Only I could change that. There was a stile at the top of the hill. Spinak and Quinn had already gone over. I changed my rhythm, moved up a gear and powered past the group of boys in front of me. Third to the stile! I stepped up on to it and for a moment wanted to sit there and rest and admire the view. But what I saw was Spinak, pounding down Bog's Field, and Quinn padding after him. There were runners close behind me. I could hear them panting and gasping. I fled down the field and felt the first splashes of icy water and cold mud splattering up my legs. Further on you could feel the mud drying like little cooked cakes on your legs. I hit puddles, ruts and bumps, and mud shot up as far as an eyelid. But I kept going. My inner voice was more placatory now. 'You're placed well; you can't just hold it, though. Try catching Quinn!'

Try catching the wind! I had to do that. Soon both of them would reach the wood and I'd lose sight of them. I didn't want that to happen. My breathing was better. I'd found a kind of rhythm, but what I needed was simply to fun faster. My legs responded. I was narrowing the gap with the leaders. I glanced over my shoulder. And I was drawing away from the others! A three-horse race?

'Don't tempt fate!' the inner voice murmured. 'There's a long way to go.'

I knew it, and by the time I reached the wood Spinak and Quinn seemed far ahead, flashes of white shorts and yellow vests glimpsed through dark trees. But I liked the run through the wood. The ground was harder. It was easier to run faster. The wind was less cruel and only occasionally stabbed like a knife. I felt warmer. I started thinking of a hot bath and Mum's Welsh rarebit. The wood was quiet, a good sign. There was no crashing behind me in the undergrowth. As long as I kept up with the pair in front, I had a chance.

I was daydreaming. A big black bird clattered from

a bare branch and screamed at my intrusion. I was slackening my stride. I was slowing up. I couldn't see or hear Quinn or Spinak. The wood was very still except when the wind moaned with loneliness and snatched at the tops of trees.

'Faster, faster! You've got to catch them up!' The inner voice was right.

I fought the lead feeling in my legs and the stitch in my side. That would pass. I was running as fast as I dared at this stage of the race. I was giving it all I'd got. I circled a clump of trees, and suddenly there they were! Quinn twenty yards ahead of me and Spinak only the same distance in front of Quinn. I'd never been this close before. Spinak glanced over his shoulder and increased his pace. Quinn stayed with him, not gaining, not losing ground. I experienced a strange moment of realization. Neither was invincible. I could win this race! I'd never really thought I could before. The wood would peter out soon, then there was a little clearing, Toll's Tunnel . . . the crescent field . . . the cinder track . . . home . . .

I staggered past Quinn. Neither of us had breath for words. I almost felt guilty! I kept up the pressure. My inner voice was deadly silent as I came running out of the wood and I was neck and neck with Spinak. Ahead of us, just across the grassy clearing, Toll's Tunnel yawned like a deep black mouth. It wasn't a man-made tunnel as such. It was a boggy lane about half a mile long. The trees and brambles on either side were so thick and dense, even in winter, that they joined above your head like grasping, interlocking fingers and hands. It was a gloomy, wet place and would be hard to run through.

I was matching Spinak stride for stride and stagger for stagger. It was a balancing act to keep my feet on rough ground. I pushed myself harder and harder and, to my gasping amazement, found I was suddenly ahead of him and entering the cavernous tunnel alone. It stretched before me, and I had the strangest sensation that I'd run from day into night, dark night, with only the hollow moaning of the wind for company. The ground was a black sea, wave after wave of water-filled ruts. I plunged on. And on. I nearly lost a sneaker. The mud was treacherous. It sucked at my feet as though to pull me down and swallow me up. I slipped and ran. On and on. Then it was darker, much darker and something was wrong. The cold wet ground was beneath my feet. My legs were moving, but *I* wasn't moving. It was like trying to run up a down escalator, or worse, I was paralysed in a nightmare.

My inner running voice was oddly silent. No words of comfort, advice or encouragement were offered. There was only the darkness and my legs, which moved yet kept me rooted to the spot. I shuddered. My body was cold as though all my blood had turned to ice. My teeth chattered. I couldn't explain it, but I was deeply afraid. How could it be so dark? Where was Spinak and Quinn and all the others? What was happening? My legs raced, and suddenly I was hurtling forward over a long, hidden stone. Pain shot from toe to chin. The ground came up to meet me. I groaned. Oh no, that was it, I'd thrown the race. I staggered to my feet and tried to run.

The pain disappeared. I was in working order! I could run . . . but I couldn't move. I was running on the spot again. I heard myself groaning with frustration and fear. I was trapped and held by an invisible force, and that wasn't possible. Tears started in my eyes. I had to escape. I called upon all my strength and energy to move me and peered into the deep gloom ahead. Molecules of darkness were crowding together as though gathered by the lonely wind. A shape formed and gained in substance. I swept at my eyes. I was seeing things. It was a man. His face was hidden behind a cloak. His voice moaned and spoke directly to my inner voice.

'So many of you. So many. And you the first. You must pay. Pay for all of them.'

I started gibbering aloud. I wasn't making sense.

'I, I haven't got money. This is a cross-country race.'

'You have disturbed me. You must pay. Pay with your blood.'

My legs pounded into the ground. Still I couldn't move. My arms raced like pistons. The man's cloak fell aside. I screamed. I was staring into the eyeless sockets of a decaying skull. Fleshless fingers clutched a gleaming dagger. The figure was advancing on me. He was over me. The knife was raised high above his skull. I lurched to one side, staggered, found my feet . . . and joy! My legs answered my call for action. They moved. I was tearing into the blackness of the tunnel.

'Just run, run for your life, that's all you can do!'

I knew it. I didn't need the inner dialogue any more. As I ran I looked over my shoulder. The figure was nearly on me. All I could do was run.

I steamed out of Toll's Tunnel into unexpected cold sunlight. The crescent field curved before me, and there was the red-haired Spinak, two or three hundred yards off, and behind him Quinn and perhaps twenty or thirty runners. I'd never catch them now. It was all over. I could hear a runner behind me. I turned my head in despair and there was no one. Only the wind moaned, and on its breath I heard those dreadful words, in that awful hollow

123

voice, 'You still haven't paid. You must pay. Pay for them all.'

A new strength and energy surged through me. The voice was on my shoulder. I remembered the dagger. I still saw its gleam. My eyes were blurred. My legs carried my body as though I was no longer a part of it. I passed a knot of boys running together. For a moment I recognized them, but from the way they looked at me I felt like a stranger. I passed Benson. He was a good runner, then there was Atkins, then Bridges. Jefferson and Dobson. So many, so many of them ahead of me. It was all too late. Then I was behind Quinn, and I could hear voices shouting and cheering. We were off the field and on to the hill which led down to the cinder track. I was powering after Quinn. There didn't seem time to catch him, but I did. I was round him and nearly sprinting down the hill. At the bottom of it I saw Spinak turn into the cinder track. Could I catch him? I heard the wind moaning. I heard voices shouting. I was on the cinder track and this was home and Spinak was ten yards in front of me. I heard somewhere my dad's voice shouting, 'Push it Danny, *push* it.' Spinak glanced over his shoulder. Could he find new legs? Could I? The tape was in sight. Faces, things were blurring. Cameras flashed. I was neck and neck with Spinak. For a moment we matched each other, step for step, breath for breath . . .

'Easy, easy, put that coat around him.' I heard Mr Relph's kindly voice, and it sounded as though it was coming from far away. I heard Dad saying congratulatory things and Mum sounding anxious. I was trying to stand upright, and they were all holding me up. Spinak pumped my hand. His voice was quavering and came in short bursts. 'You came . . .

like a bat . . . out of hell . . . Took me at the tape . . .'

'Toll's Tunnel,' I panted.

'Saw you stuck in the mud there,' Quinn said with a chuckle. 'Thought you were finished.'

'I nearly was,' I said.

'I think we'll have to go back to the old route in future,' Mr Relph said. 'Too many boys lost shoes there. It's too boggy.'

'And the ghost of the old toll-keeper,' I blurted out.

Mr Relph laughed. 'Oh, that's an old story, Danny. Ghosts are all in the mind. It's your training that paid off today. You finally realized your full potential. Next step is the county championships.'

I couldn't help but beam with pleasure then. But Mr Relph was right and he was also wrong. My training had paid off, but not all ghosts are in the mind. One of them exists in Toll's Tunnel. I know. I saw it. I ran for my life. And that's the only piece of advice I'd give to anyone foolish enough to pass through that gloomy place: run for your life!

THE CAT ROOM

R. Chetwynd-Hayes

When the Goodridge family moved into Balaclava Cottage, Sabrina lost no time in exploring the empty rooms, leaving her parents to supervise the furniture removal men, who kept enquiring: 'Where do you want this, ma'am?' and 'Where shall we put the what-not, ma'am?'

The 'cottage' had six rooms upstairs and six down, a fact that caused Mrs Goodridge grave concern, for she had shaken her head several times and expressed doubt that she could keep such a barn of a place clean.

'My great-uncle managed all right,' Mr Goodridge pointed out, 'and he only had a charlady in three times a week.'

'Yes, and a fine old mess it was, too,' Mrs Goodridge said, 'Still, he left the place to you, and we mustn't look a gift horse in the mouth. Vanman, that sofa goes in the front parlour.'

Sabrina ran up the stairs and began opening doors, peering into bedrooms and trying to decide which one she would like for herself. The large master bedroom would obviously be used by her parents and was, in fact, already fitted with an almost new Axminster carpet, of which her mother was vastly proud. But a much smaller room, situated at the back of the house, had two deep cupboards, a fascinating little iron fireplace and faded wallpaper with a most unusual pattern. It had a yellow background and rows of black cats' heads that ran diagonally across the paper, creating the impression that they had sprung out of the ceiling and were sliding down behind the wainscoting.

Sabrina had never seen wallpaper that had looked even remotely like this and decided that this room must be hers.

'What!' Mr Goodridge was trying to move a sideboard that refused to go against the dining-room wall. 'Those cat-heads will drive you crazy.'

'No, they won't. Daddy, all my life I've wanted a room with cat-heads on the wallpaper. Never – never have I wanted anything so much.'

'Well . . . you'd better ask your mother.'

Mrs Goodridge was watching the removal men with a critical eye as they carried a sofa into the sitting-room and did not view the idea with any great enthusiasm.

'But I wanted you to have the room next to ours. Frankly, that awful wallpaper gives me the shivers. I want your father to strip it off and paint the walls with a nice pink emulsion.'

'But all of my life I've wanted . . .'

'Don't be silly.'

'*Please*. I'll clean all of the windows once a week if you'll let me have that room.'

Mrs Goodridge flinched when one of the men bumped an armchair against a door-frame.

'Oh, very well. I suppose I'll get no peace until you have your way. But don't blame me if you have horrid dreams.'

Once the 'cat room' – which was Sabrina's own name for her new retreat – was furnished, it did look rather cosy. Her brass bedstead, complete with bright yellow spread, stood against the wall facing the window; bookcases seemed to smile benignly at the wardrobe, which nestled snugly beside the old fire-place recess, and the pretty frills of her dressing-table brightened a dark corner. When the pink-shaded bed-side lamp was switched on, all the cat-heads on the walls appeared to grin with unstinted appreciation.

'Not bad.' Mrs Goodridge nodded her reluctant approval. 'But I'm still not happy about that wall-paper. The old man must have been mad.'

Mr Goodridge grinned and switched on the over-head light.

'Eccentric, maybe. But he was a clever commercial artist. Probably designed that wallpaper himself.'

'Pity he couldn't have found a more useful way of spending his time,' Mrs Goodridge observed causti-cally. 'Sabrina, wash your hands. Dinner will soon be ready.'

It was two weeks before Balaclava Cottage acquired that 'lived in' atmosphere which is an absolute necess-ity before a house can be called a home. During that period extra furniture had to be purchased, fitted carpet laid in the hall and curtains made for most of the windows. Sabrina helped her father cut the grass, pull weeds from the sadly neglected garden and paint the front door a lovely emerald green.

Then the nights began to draw in and the moon grew until it looked like a large ripe orange.

Sabrina woke up suddenly. One moment she was in a deep, dreamless sleep – the next wide awake, every sense alert, trying to determine what it was that had disturbed her. She raised her head and looked across the room. A full moon had transformed the window curtains into a silver screen, made the darkness retreat into corners, created slabs of shadow that lay before the bookcase and wardrobe, and turned the dressing-table mirror into a vast gleaming eye. A night breeze crept in through the partly open window and stirred the curtains, making it seem as if all the cat-heads on the wallpaper were opening and closing their mouths, as though sending out silent cries.

Then Sabrina heard the sound.

A low growl. She felt an icy wave of fear creep up from her feet and create chilly butterflies in her stomach, as she sat up and fumbled for the bedside lamp switch. Light exploded and shattered the silver gloom, sent out a pink-tinted radiance that formed a rough circle round the bed and was reflected in the wardrobe mirror.

The growl was repeated, only now it came from the region of the dressing-table. Sabrina strained her eyes, anxious to discover what caused this alarming noise, but at the same time terrified of what she might see. Suddenly she became aware of two little spots of yellow light that came round from behind the dressing-table and advanced into the room. Sabrina's hand flew to her mouth and she choked back a scream as an extremely large cat emerged into the circle of pink light. She had never seen such a cat before: long black fur that stood on end, ears laid back flat on either side of the round head, an open mouth that revealed long, pointed teeth, and eyes that glittered like polished amber discs. A long tail lashed from side to side.

The cat crept slowly forward, crouched low so that its stomach brushed the carpet. It stopped on reaching a position to the left of Sabrina's bed and looked up at her with hate-filled eyes. The growl rose to a terrifying howl. Sabrina, more frightened than at any time in her life, said the first words that came into her head.

'Nice puss . . . mice . . . milk . . .'

The sound of her voice seemed partially to reassure the cat, for the pointed ears made an attempt to become upright, the tail ceased its angry lashing and the eyes blinked. Then, as though ashamed of a momentary weakness, the black cat turned, went back on to its hindquarters and jumped towards the mantelpiece.

It disappeared in mid-air.

After a few moments spent in trying to come to terms with this alarming phenomenon, Sabrina remembered her voice again – and screamed.

'That awful wallpaper!' Mrs Goodridge exclaimed for the seventh time. 'I knew it would give her night-mares, but no one paid any attention to me. It doesn't take an ounce of commonsense to know that rows of cats' heads will do something to a child's mind.'

'But, Mummy,' Sabrina insisted, 'it wasn't a dream. The black cat was really there. And it did disappear.'

Mr Goodridge of course did his best to be practical and line up a number of indisputable facts in a neat row.

'Now,' he said heartily, 'let's put on our thinking caps. First, we haven't got a cat. Secondly, all the doors were locked, and the windows – was your window open, Sabrina?'

'Only a tiny bit,' said Sabrina. 'I don't think a kitten could have got in, let alone such a monster cat. It was huge!'

'Thirdly, then,' went on Mr Goodridge, 'even if a cat did manage somehow to get in, it couldn't poss-ibly have disappeared in mid-air. Therefore you must have had a nasty dream. I remember once dreaming about a donkey . . .'

130

'But it could have been a ghost-cat,' Sabrina pointed out. 'A very unhappy ghost-cat.'

Mrs Goodridge sat down and gave the impression she would faint, if given the least encouragement.

'Did you hear, Clarence? The poor child's deranged! A ghost-cat! She thinks the place is haunted!'

'A fertile imagination, my dear,' said Mr Goodridge comfortingly. 'Takes after my side of the family, I shouldn't wonder. Now, I propose that Sabrina spends the rest of the night in one of the spare rooms and we all try to get some sleep. Tomorrow, we can decide what's to be done.'

'It wasn't a dream and it wasn't imagination!' Sabrina announced angrily, exasperated – not for the first time – by the gross stupidity that is so often displayed by even the nicest of adults. 'I saw a ghost-cat, and I believe there's a reason why it's haunting that room.'

Next morning, Mrs Coggins arrived. She was tall and thin and wore a faded overall and plimsolls. She nodded her head in Mrs Goodridge's direction.

'I used to come and oblige for the old gentleman, madam, and I wondered if I could come and oblige you.'

Mrs Goodridge patted her forehead with a lace handkerchief. 'Oblige? I don't understand.'

'Do for him, madam. Do the housework, like. Me charges are quite moderate, and if you asks me to have a 'ot dinner, I won't say no.'

'It might be a good idea,' Mr Goodridge suggested, 'as this house is much larger than our old one. And if this good lady could char . . .'

'Oblige,' Mrs Coggins corrected.

'Yes, quite . . . oblige for a few hours a week, it would make things easier for you.'

Mrs Goodridge waved her handkerchief as a gesture depicting temporary helplessness.

'I'm certainly fit for nothing after last night. Let her remain by all means. Can she cook?'

Mrs Coggins frowned and drew herself upright.

'The name is Coggins, madam, and I can cook. Nothing fancy, but good wholesome fare such as the old gentleman found to his liking. If you feel poorly, just go upstairs and lie down and leave everything to me. I prefers not to have any interference.'

'I'm not at all certain . . .' Mrs Goodridge began, but her husband took her firmly by one arm and propelled her towards the stairs.

'Don't worry, dear. I'm sure Mrs Coggins will manage nicely, and Sabrina can make herself useful with the washing-up and so forth.'

With some reluctance, Mrs Goodridge allowed herself to be led upstairs, and Sabrina, who suddenly realized that she now had a source of information regarding her great-great-uncle – and even, possibly, the ghost-cat as well – carried a pile of plates into the kitchen, then grabbed a wiping-up towel.

'You show willing, I'll say that for you,' Mrs Coggins remarked, rolling up her sleeves. 'Which is more than can be said for most kids these days. Mind you don't break any of your mother's china.'

For a while Sabrina busied herself with wiping plates and piling them on to the dresser. Then she asked:

'Did you work for my great-great-uncle for long?'

Mrs Coggins nodded. 'Yus, I obliged the old gentleman for nigh on ten years.'

'Was . . . was he a strange man?'

'I don't know about strange. He kept himself to himself, which I didn't hold against him.'

'Did he ever have a cat?'

'Not that I'm aware of. Of course there was that room that he'd never let me into, and I suppose he could have kept a cat in there. Certainly I once caught a glimpse of that outlandish wallpaper, and that must mean he liked 'em. Still – what's the harm? Lots of people like cats.'

'I do agree,' Sabrina hastened to reassure the old woman. 'I like them myself.'

Mrs Coggins placed a kettle on the gas stove.

'Mind you, there's them that say things went on in this house, that weren't right or proper for a honest Christian, but I never saw anything out of the way.'

Sabrina curbed a wave of excitement and waited until all of the china had been placed in the dresser before she spoke again.

'What sort of things – these things that went on?'

Mrs Coggins poured boiling water into a brown earthenware pot, then emptied it into the sink.

'Remember – always heat the pot. What sort of things? None that need concern you. Warlock, indeed!'

'What's a warlock?' Sabrina asked.

'A man witch. Stuff and nonsense! Now, let's have a nice cup of tea and don't you go asking me any more questions. I've got work to do.'

Sabrina decided that no more information could be obtained from the old woman and presently made her way to the small room that Mr Goodridge had commandeered as a study. She removed a large dictionary from the bookcase and turned the pages over until she found the word *Warlock*.

'A wizard, sorcerer, magician,' she read aloud. 'A man in league with, or under the influence of, evil spirits; male follower of the black art. A familiar in the shape of a black cat was said to relay orders from the devil to the warlock or witch.'

Sabrina closed the dictionary and leaned back in her father's swivel chair. The prospect that her bedroom was haunted by a ghost-cat that acted as messenger boy for the Devil was an exceedingly frightening one, but – when considered in broad daylight – rather exciting. However, if her great-great-uncle had been a warlock, she was certain the black cat had performed his satanic duties with great reluctance and now wanted to be set free, so he could go to wherever cats go when they die. She didn't know how she knew this – it was just something she felt sure about. After some rather fearful deliberation, Sabrina came to a heart-thumping decision. She was going to have a shot at laying the ghost-cat.

At two o'clock next morning – an hour when it was reasonable to suppose her parents were fast asleep – Sabrina crept over the dark landing, opened the door of the haunted room, then, after switching on the ceiling lamp, closed the door carefully behind her. The room still looked as cosy and unhaunted as anyone could wish for, and the girl began to wonder if her terrifying experience, had, after all, been nothing more than an exceptionally vivid dream. Then she remembered the upright fur, the glaring eyes, and knew she had been fully awake, and no amount of self-deception could alter the fact. But how did one set about laying a ghost-cat?

Sabrina sat on her bed and gave the matter full consideration. Surely the first question that demanded an answer was – what made the cat appear? There was certainly no sign of it at present, which suggested that either the conditions were not favourable, or the apparition only appeared at a certain time. Sabrina tried to remember everything that had happened prior to hearing that terrifying growl. She had woken up and found the room bathed in moonlight, then she had switched on the bedside lamp. But . . . but the window had been slightly open, and the breeze was disturbing the curtains . . . and all the cat-heads on the wallpaper seemed to be opening and closing their mouths. Sabrina gulped and tried very hard not to be frightened.

The wallpaper . . . the wallpaper was the key! No wonder she had thought it to be so enthralling. Moonlight . . . waving curtains . . . dancing shadows . . . all doing something horrible to the wallpaper.

'Gosh!' Sabrina whispered, astonished at a thought that had just come to her. 'Maybe there never was a real cat at all! Perhaps it's a sort of extension of my great-great-uncle.'

She sat for some time looking at the wallpaper, and now it did appear to be very sinister indeed. Every cat-head seemed to have acquired yellow, glaring eyes, each open mouth gave the impression that it might produce a growl at any moment, and all appeared to be three-dimensional – straining to get off the wallpaper. Sabrina spoke again, deriving some small comfort from the sound of her own voice.

'I don't really want to – I'll be scared silly – but I must know.'

She got up and switched off the overhead lamp, then walked over to the window and opened it a fraction. The moon – as though waiting for such a signal – obligingly slid from behind a cloud and bathed the room in silver light. Sabrina slowly turned round and took up a position against the left hand wall. The curtains stirred and cast flimsy shadows over the wallpaper. Instantly, the cat-heads opened their mouths, while their eyes glittered like flickering stars on a frosty night.

Then, from behind the dressing-table came a distinct low growl, and the black cat crept into view, looking even larger and more ferocious than Sabrina remembered. It came forward with stomach brushing the carpet, ears laid back, fur standing on end, and stopped a few feet from the trembling girl.

The head went back, the immense eyes became pools of yellow fire, and the humped shoulders quivered as though the creature was about to leap. Suddenly the door opened, and Mr Goodridge, attired in a flower-patterned dressing-gown, entered. He said: 'I thought as much . . .' then stopped, his eyes bulging when the ghost-cat spun round with one swift movement and faced the intruder. Sabrina did her best to speak calmly.

'Daddy, please turn the light on – quickly.'

'What . . . what in the name of sanity is it?'

'The ghost-cat. Please turn on the light, then I think it will jump towards the mantelpiece and disappear.'

Mr Goodridge took what seemed to be a long time fumbling for the light switch, but finally the lamp sprang into life, smothering the moonlight under a soft pink glow. Immediately the black cat turned and raced around the bed with incredible speed. When it reached the hearth-rug, it went back on its haunches, leapt towards the mantel-shelf and vanished in mid air.

For the space of several seconds neither father nor daughter spoke, then Mr Goodridge whispered:

'Thank God your mother's not awake. But I couldn't sleep, and I heard you creeping across the landing. A ghost-cat! Great heavens!'

Sabrina, whose courage had now revived, closed the window, then said: 'I think it's not only the wallpaper, but something behind the chimney breast. I mean, why else should the ghost-cat jump towards it and disappear?'

Mr. Goodridge gave the fireplace an apprehensive glance.

'Don't ask me. I never reckoned on anything like this when I took the house over. What your mother will say when she finds out there really is a ghost-cat doesn't bear thinking about. Want to move, I shouldn't wonder.'

'If,' Sabrina said slyly, 'we were to clear the matter up tonight, she need never know. Let's examine that fireplace and see what we can find out.'

Her father looked anxiously around the room.

'I suppose there's no chance of that thing coming back? I don't think I could face it again.'

Sabrina crossed her fingers and gave what she hoped was the correct reply.

'No, of course not. One appearance a night is all it has – has strength for. Now, let's look at the fireplace.'

It was she who bent down and put her head into the opening and peered up the chimney. One thing was certain, a fire could never be lit in the grate, for the chimney had been bricked up, and, if the newness of the brickwork was anything to go by, quite recently, too.

She straightened up and ran an exploring hand over the chimney-breast. The surface was smooth, but when she tapped the wall there was a hollow sound in an area about one foot square, just above the shelf.

'I knew I was right,' she informed a still very disturbed Mr Goodridge. 'There's a small cupboard

137

built into the chimney space. If you were to get a hammer and chisel, we could have it open in no time.'

'Perhaps tomorrow morning,' her father suggested.

'When mummy will want to know what you are doing?'

'I won't be a moment. My tool kit is in one of the spare rooms.'

While she was waiting, Sabrina tore away a strip of the wallpaper.

A shudder seemed to run round the entire room, and she jumped back. Zig-zag cracks appeared on all four walls, and the cat-heads began to fade. Presently, they took on the appearance of grey splodges. From behind the chimney-breast, Sabrina heard the distinct sound of a long-drawn-out sigh.

Mr Goodridge returned, carrying a large tool bag. He stopped just inside of the door and looked around in amazement.

'What's happened to that awful wallpaper?'

Sabrina gave what she thought was a feasible answer.

'I tore some and sort of wounded the room. Well – that's the only way I can describe it. Look – there's a plain wooden panel here. All you've got to do is prise it out – then we'll see.'

The panel surrendered after Mr Goodridge had given it a few quiet taps with his hammer and chisel; it came away with a sharp, cracking sound – and revealed a dark recess. Mr Goodridge – after some hesitation – slid his right hand into the recess and brought out a small object: a grotesque image of the ghost-cat, complete with black fur and glittering eyes that seemed to be alive with hate or fear. He examined it with lively interest.

'It's quite heavy. I'd say bear skin over plaster. Let's see what else there is.'

He reached into the opening again and this time produced a roll of parchment, which he carried over to the dressing-table and laid out flat. Sabrina looked over her father's shoulder and read the following script, which had been written with a broad-nibbed pen and red ink. At least, she hoped it was red ink.

Extra from 'Unnatural Enmities and Their
Retainment'
by
Conrad Von Holstein

Make ye an image in the likeness of Ye Black Cat of Set *and place it in a confined space. Then prepare a room with the same likeness depicted on all walls from floor to ceiling, each likeness to be not less than one hand's breadth from the next, all the while chanting the incantations prepared by the immortal Macradotus. Thus shall ye – when the time be right – be given power such as few men enjoy, and whatsoever worldly goods ye desire shall be yours. But be warned. Should death creep upon ye unawares, and the image be not destroyed, then shall ye walk the night hours on four feet, until that thing is done which ye left undone.*

Mr Goodridge took one long look at the open recess, the cracked wallpaper that was now beginning to peel from the walls, and finally at the cat image that lay on the bed. He sighed and said:

'Well, I guess I'll do that which was left undone. This cat thing and the piece of paper are going into the boiler – right now. And let's hope that's the end of the ghost-cat.'

It was. And before long the 'cat-room' became the

'pink room', when Mr Goodridge gave the walls several coats of rose-coloured emulsion.

'Very nice, Clarence,' said Mrs Goodridge. 'And much more suitable than cats, Sabrina, don't you think?'

THE HAUNTERS
Mary Danby

Each year, ten members of the Westhampton Boys' Club were invited to spend a weekend as the guests of Mr and Mrs Theodore Portly in their Georgian mansion. These visits to Blackwood Hall were enormously popular, not least because there were rumours that the Ancestors' Gallery, as it was known, was haunted.

Jack and Bill Simpson were among the visitors to Blackwood Hall one year. Between them, they had a collection of thirty ghost books, and to see a real live ghost – or 'a real dead ghost', as Jack put it – was their greatest ambition. Accordingly, Simpson and Simpson, Ghost Hunters Extraordinary, chose a moment after supper on the first day to corner Mr Portly and ask him about the Ancestors' Gallery. They had already seen the gallery, and even by daylight it had looked strange and shadowy, its oak-panelled walls lined with Portly portraits dating back to the time the house was built. A fifteenth-century suit of armour stood to attention at one end, as though its first owner, Sir Cuthbert Portly, were still inside.

'Can't say I've seen any ghosts myself,' said Mr Portly, 'but perhaps I'm not the ghost-seeing type.'

He seemed more of a money-making type. The two seldom coincided, in the boys' experience.

'My wife, though,' he continued, 'she heard a bit of a whooshing noise once – '

'What sort of whooshing?' interrupted Bill. 'Like wind, do you mean?'

'More like whooshing, she said.' Mr Portly held a match to his cigar. 'Like somebody pretending to be a ghost.'

'And was it, do you think?' Jack asked. 'Someone pretending, that is?'

Mr Portly sucked on the cigar, examined the end of it, and lit another match.

'What I think,' he said slowly, 'is that it's time I had a large whisky. Off you go, boys, and join the others. There's a nice game of ping-pong going on in the hall, by the sound of it.'

Bill groaned, but Jack nudged him in the ribs. 'Er, Mr Portly,' he called after the plump figure edging towards the drawing-room, 'just one more question?'

Their host seemed to sag a little, but stopped politely. 'Yes?'

'If there *is* a ghost, and it's a real one, have you any idea who it could have been?'

'Not the slightest,' said Mr Portly.

There was only one thing to do. That night, when the house was in darkness, the two boys left the bedroom they were sharing and made their way towards the Ancestors' Gallery. They slipped past the Portlys' bedroom, stifling their giggles at the sound of rumbling snores, and crept through the library, with its ceiling-high shelves of leather-bound books.

'Bet they've never even been read,' whispered Bill. 'Imagine having to wade your way through that lot.'

'Ssh,' replied Jack, opening the door at the other end.

The gallery was even more menacing by moonlight. The portraits seemed to stare and mock, as if sharing a private joke against the boys. Jack and Bill stayed close together, their shoulders touching, and waited.

'Perhaps it's not the ghost's night,' suggested Jack. 'Perhaps it – '

He stopped short as a noise came from one of the window-seats at the side of the gallery. 'Ooo-ooo-ooo,' it went.

'The ghost!' hissed Bill.

Then a white shape stepped from behind a curtain and slowly raised its arms.

'That's it,' said Jack. 'I'm off!'

They raced through the library, past the now-hiccuping snores and back to their bedroom. Bill collapsed on to his bed and sat on his hands to stop them shaking.

'Oh crikey, oh help, ooh-er,' he kept saying.

But Jack was pacing up and down, punching his fists together and mumbling to himself. 'It must be,' he said. 'If that wasn't someone dressed up in a sheet and trying to scare us out of our wits, I'm a blue-nosed banana.'

'Y-you're a w-what?' Bill's teeth were chattering.

'Look, it was one of the others. Dave, or Tony, or one of that lot. They overheard us planning our ghost-hunt and thought they'd have a laugh. Any fool could see it was someone wearing a sheet.'

Bill had to admit he was right. After all, real ghosts are kind of filmy. They waft. They don't tread firmly out from behind curtains.

'Well then,' Jack said. 'We'd better see who has the last laugh.'

The next day they were careful to make sure everyone knew their plans.

'We thought we might investigate the ghost tonight,' Jack said casually. 'Around midnight.'

'In the gallery, you know,' added Bill.

At five minutes to twelve, they left their bedroom, looking carefully around to see if any of the other doors were opening. Both were carrying sheets.

'We'll see who's afraid of ghosts now,' said Jack as he opened the door to the gallery. 'Quick. On with your sheet.'

The two draped figures made their way to the nearest window-seat and each hid behind a curtain. They heard the clock in the hall below them strike twelve. Slowly, the door from the library opened.

'Now,' whispered Jack.

Bill began making what he thought was a ghostly noise. 'Ooo-woo,' he went. 'Whoooooosh-woooo.'

Jack peeped out from behind the curtain. Sure enough, another white-sheeted figure was advancing on them.

'Whooooo-er, boooooo,' went Bill.

'Whoooosh,' went the newcomer.

'Blast, we haven't scared him,' muttered Jack. He moved out from the window-seat and stood with his arms raised in the middle of the gallery, trying to look spectral. The newcomer moved nearer, also raising its arms.

'O.K.,' said Jack. 'Who are you? Is it you, Tony?'

'Whooooooooooo,' said the newcomer, even louder.

Bill came out of his hiding place and stood beside Jack. 'It's not fair,' he said. 'He's got a bigger sheet. Mine's so small you can see my pyjama legs.'

'Shut up,' said Jack fiercely.

'But it's only a joke,' began Bill.

The newcomer was just a few feet from them now, and still advancing.

'Look, you can stop now.' Jack's voice was beginning to tremble. 'You've – you've had your fun.'

It was Bill who screamed first. He realized, before it happened, that the thing in the sheet was going to walk right through him. Jack screamed when he felt the icy clamminess of nothing around him, turning his blood to water. Two hands clutched their hearts with fingers of cold menace, and the last thing they heard was a chuckling 'whooooooosh'.

They stood with Peregrine, for that was the name of their new-found friend, at the library window, watching their funeral procession setting off for the church. It was gratifying to see how sad everyone looked.

'Did you watch your own funeral?' Bill asked Peregrine.

'Most certainly, old sport,' replied the white sheet next to him. 'It was most enjoyable. Of course, there were some who said I had been asking for trouble, dressing up like this to frighten Lady Blatherstone, but it was a fearfully good wheeze – even if I did trip on my sheet and impale myself on Sir Cuthbert's battle-axe.'

'What do we do now?' said Jack.

Peregrine considered the situation. 'For a start,' he said, 'I could give you some haunting lessons.' He turned to Bill. 'That 'Ooo-woo' of yours, for instance, was a little jerky. Try it after me. Ooooo-woooo. Like that. Nice and smooth.'

'Ooooo-woooo.'

'Better, old bean. Much better. Again, please.'

The next year, six members of the boys' club team were thrown into quivering panic by the sight of three white-sheeted figures whooshing their way down the Ancestors' Gallery.

Back in one of the bedrooms, the boldest among them, Sam Coggins, said: 'You needn't think a few boys in white sheets can scare me. No, sir. Come on, let's do a little haunting ourselves.' He chuckled. 'We'll see who has the last laugh.'

Three echoes wafted past the door. A kind of chortling 'whoosh', a groaning 'aargh' – and a very smooth 'oooo-woooo'.

DEVIL HORSE
Patricia Leitch

'How absolutely super,' said Peter, my elder brother.

'How utterly dreadful,' I said.

We were both standing in the garden of our holiday cottage. We had just arrived and our parents were too busy unpacking the car to pay any attention to us. They were fed up listening to me, anyway. I hadn't wanted to come on holiday with my family. I had wanted to go with Liz and Suzy, my two best friends, to a very posh riding establishment for a fortnight's show-jumping course. It had almost been arranged when Daddy discovered the cost.

'One hundred pounds a week!' he had exclaimed, going into instant shock. 'Most certainly not.'

So here I was, stuck out in the wilds of Scotland for a fortnight's holiday in an ancient stone cottage surrounded by absolutely nothing. And I am not exaggerating when I say nothing.

Peter is mad keen on bird watching, so are my parents, which is probably why they picked the wretched cottage in the first place. Standing at the back door there was nothing to be seen but marsh, stretching around the cottage garden like an ocean.

'Look!' cried Mummy, pointing upwards and almost dropping the bags she was carrying. 'A kestrel!'

Daddy and Peter both stared enthusiastically upwards. I kept my eyes fixed on the ground.

'It is the most barren, miserable dump that I've

ever seen,' I said, and shivered suddenly as I spoke. 'There could be anything in that swamp.'

'Witches, warlocks and kelpies,' suggested Daddy, humouring me.

'Kelpies?' I asked.

'Devil horses that lurk in lonely places in the Highlands, usually by a river.'

'Or a marsh,' interrupted Peter, laughing with a hollow, haunting sound.

'And when a human comes up to them they lure him on to their backs, then ride off into the river with him, sink under the water and devour him.'

'What stupid nonsense,' I said sharply. 'I don't believe a word of it.' But I couldn't stop myself shuddering again. 'I wouldn't care what the horse was like, as long as I could have a ride on it.'

Inside, the rooms were small and poky. Peter and my parents were to sleep upstairs while I was to have the bedroom downstairs.

'It's like a matchbox,' I said in disgust when I saw it. 'I'm sure the ad said the cottage slept six. There must be another bedroom somewhere.'

'Have a look,' Mummy suggested. 'There are so many twisting passages we could easily have missed it.'

It took me five minutes to discover the other bedroom. The door leading to it was hidden by a heavy curtain. I pulled it back and unlatched the door. It led to a passage that seemed more modern than the rest of the cottage, and then to another door. I unlatched it and had to step up a high step before I was in the room. The walls were the original rough stone and the ceiling had its original wooden beams; all had been painted white. There were twin beds and a modern bedroom suite. The two side walls had small windows set into the thick stone, but the end wall had been replaced by a double-glazed French window. I walked across and stared through it. There was nothing but the sea of marsh. Again the shivery feeling tickled my spine and for a second I almost thought I would go back to my matchbox.

That evening, when we were all sitting round the table after a late supper, there was a knock on the door. Daddy answered it and brought an old woman into the kitchen. She had a shawl over her head, shielding a face brown and wrinkled as a walnut; her worn tweed skirt came down to her ankles.

'Mrs Thompson,' said Daddy, introducing her.

Dimly I remembered the name. The cottage belonged to an English family who lived in Surrey. They only used it in September; the rest of the year it was rented out to holiday-makers. Mrs Thompson looked after it for them, cleaning it between visitors and that sort of thing.

Mrs Thompson and Mummy chatted about Calor gas and hot water and milk deliveries, while I wondered what Liz and Suzy would be doing. After a bit, Mrs Thompson said she would have to be going and set off for the back door, then she stopped suddenly.

'Och, I was almost forgetting the very thing I came for. Being only the four of you you'll not be using that old room, so I'll lock it safe for you. Better that way.'

Taking a bunch of keys from her pocket she toddled off to the living-room.

'Where is she going?' asked Daddy, baffled.

Mummy shrugged her shoulders and followed Mrs Thompson. Then I heard heavy curtains being drawn back, followed by the sound of a key being turned.

'Hey!' I yelled. 'She's locking the door to my bedroom!' And I ran through to the living-room.

'Don't lock my door!' I cried. 'That's where I'm sleeping.'

But Mrs Thompson had already locked it and was putting the key back into her pocket.

'You'll not be needing it,' she said severely. 'Only the four of you. Just you be sleeping in the croft itself. Now that I've locked the door that old room won't be troubling you.'

'Jane is sleeping in there,' said Mummy.

'We've rented the whole cottage,' Daddy said, 'and our letter from the Wynne-Elliots clearly states that there is sleeping accommodation for six.'

Unwillingly, Mrs Thompson brought the key out of her pocket again. She scowled up at us from under her shawl, her eyes glaring from its shadows and her mouth clenched.

'If you would,' said Daddy, which meant: at once, or else.

Mrs Thompson unlocked the door, then she turned round and stomped back through to the kitchen. She opened the back door, and I thought she was going to march off in the huff, but at the last moment she turned to face us.

'There's no lassie of mine would sleep in that room,' she told us. 'It's not fit for a Christian soul to be in. And that's the truth I'm telling you. Falling to pieces it was, until they came here with their foolishness, tarting it up and calling it a bedroom. All the white paint in the world wouldn't cover over what was done there.' And she stomped out, banging the door behind her.

'Well!' exclaimed Peter. 'Mad as a hatter.'

'Wonder what did happen in there.' said Daddy curiously. 'They don't half hang on to their past, these Scotties.'

I can't say I slept very well that night, but then

you don't, in a strange room, in a strange bed. As I lay, trying to sleep, my imagination got going on all the things that could have happened there to make Mrs Thompson scared of it.

I woke very early in grey cold light. Going to the window I stared out at an underwater world of mist. All the marsh was swallowed up in shrouds of grey vapour. I watched, fascinated, as the early sun began to move the mist, making it flow and spiral with shafts of light. Then suddenly I was sure I'd seen a black horse, rearing and galloping through the mist. No horse could graze on that swamp, I thought. He must have escaped from somewhere. But the mists had closed again and I couldn't see him any more. He must have strayed, I thought, struggling into jeans, sweater and sandals. I wrenched open the heavy glass door and ran out into the garden.

I ran across the weed-grown lawn, scrambled over the wooden fence and I was in the marsh. The clumps of tufted reeds rose to my shoulders, and my feet oozed in icy water. I had no idea what I was going to do, for I hadn't a halter. I think I just wanted to see the horse and somehow find out who owned him, in the hopes of making horsy friends for the holidays.

This way and that I plunged my way through the marsh shouting, 'Whoa!' and 'Steady boy!' into the mist. At last, when I had tripped full length and was covered from head to toe with mucky water, I gave up. I stood staring about me into the blinding mist.

It was then I heard the whinny – a brazen, stallion scream of terror from somewhere out in the marsh. Suddenly I felt nervous. I glanced quickly over my shoulder and could just make out the cottage fence. A duck flew out of a clump of reeds close by me and, in an instant, I had swung round and was plunging back to the cottage.

The next afternoon I was walking home from the village when I saw Mrs Thompson on the road in front of me. She might know who the horse belongs to, I thought, and I hurried to catch up with her.

'Good afternoon,' I said, but she didn't look up.

'Could I carry your bag for you?' I offered, but she only clung more tightly to her shopper.

'I was wondering,' I said, still walking beside her, 'If you might know who the horse belongs to that was galloping on the marsh this morning. A black horse, I think he was.'

If my other remarks had had no effect on her, she made up for it now, dropping her bag where she stood, she crossed herself, muttering violently under her breath.

'So you've seen him,' she stated, her black eyes beetling up at me.

'Well, it was very misty . . .' I begun.

'Did I not warn your mother to keep you from that room? That he should have come to one so young. The Devil himself, he is. Now you be taking the warning of an old woman and don't be going into that room again. Be sending your father to take your things from it, and it is myself will come to lock it secure for you.'

'What are you talking about?' I demanded in astonishment. 'It was only a horse, for goodness' sake.'

'Did you hear the whinny?' Mrs Thompson asked in a voice of doom.

'Yes,' I said, and she crossed herself again.

'They all hear it,' she stated grimly.

'Do stop making such a mystery out of it,' I said crossly. 'What did happen to make you so spooky about my room?'

'Listen you, then, and I'll be telling you. It was on Hallowe'en eve, over a hundred years ago. The croft belonged to a blacksmith by the name of James Baird, and a God-fearing man he was, too. God rest his soul. That room you are sleeping in, it was the smithy itself.'

'Gosh!' I exclaimed, 'was it really?' but she ignored me.

'And it was in that very room at his own forge the man was working with the gloom deepening and the mists coming in from the marsh. On that night the stranger came to the smithy. Garbed all in black, he was, and leading a stallion, black as the night itself. The beast was needing shod. Not a trace of a shoe did it have on it, it being well kent that the Devil's tribe cannot stand the breath of the cold iron, and if they would have their beasts shod they must come to ask aid of a human. The stranger left the brute tied to the smithy wall, saying he would collect him when the work was done. One man passed by and saw the great beast tied there, not fretting like a horse of flesh and blood, but standing with never a movement from it, only its great neck arched and its eyes fixed on the smith, waiting its time.'

Despite the warm sunny afternoon I shivered, goose over my grave, and looked around, longing to see Peter coming down the road to meet me.

'Now the wife of the smith was out at night. She came back with neighbours, and as they approached the smithy they heard a great crashing which sent them all running to discover the cause. And then, as they came to the croft, they heard a scream of the beast. When they reached the smithy, they saw by the glow of the forge the smith lying in a huddled shape on the floor with the great horse of hell rearing over him. The brute heard them and came straight at them, leaping clear over their heads with a stench of brimstone, and was gone into the night.'

'How terrible,' I said. 'Was the blacksmith all right?'

'Stone dead he was, with the great crescent hoof-print on his head, and he lies now in the graveyard on the hill. When they found the horse roaming the marsh they shot it and left it to sink, and the minister himself putting a horseshoe at the place to keep him there . . . But never a sign of the stranger. And since that night there's not a one would live in that haunted place.'

'They do now,' I said, trying to clear my head and bring back a little normality to the conversation. 'The cottage is taken for the whole summer. We were lucky to get it.'

'None who have sense would stay in it,' said the old woman, and I could feel her glee and her eyes watching me to see if she had scared me. 'Shall I be coming with you now to lock the door?'

'Oh, good gracious no!' I exclaimed, certain that I wasn't going to let her see that I was afraid. 'I love horses.' And to my great relief I saw Peter coming down the road. 'Here's my brother. I'll have to go. Thanks for the fairy tale.'

When I told my family, they were sceptical and more interested in a golden eagle they had seen, although Mummy did suggest that I should return to the matchbox.

That night I lay awake, trying to imagine what the smithy had been like; where the forge had been, where the smith had lain dead and where the ring had been where the black stallion had stood tied to the wall. Then there was a sudden crash of metal and the scream of a stallion. I sat bolt upright, straining my ears, but all was silent again, with the intense

154

silence of the marsh by night. When I awoke in the morning I was still sitting propped up against the headboard and not sure whether I had dreamt it or not.

I went through for breakfast meaning to tell my family, but somehow I didn't. I had been scared, but more curious than scared, and if Mummy discovered that I had been imagining things, as she would have called it, she would have insisted that I returned to the matchbox.

I heard nothing more of the horse until the Monday of our second week. It was a very hot night and I had left the curtains open. I woke up during the night sure there was something outside the window. I stared out, and the black shadows moved. My heart thumped in my throat. I was sure a huge horse was standing there – neck crested, eyes glistening. Or was it only moving shadows? But I was certain it was a horse. If it had been anything other than a horse I would have been screaming for help, but I couldn't really be afraid of a horse, even a ghost killer-horse – not of any horse. I loved all horses.

I ran to the window, and as I reached it there was a crash of metal and the high-pitched whinny. Yet there was nothing at the window. Suddenly I wondered if Mrs Thompson was making it all up, if really I was only imagining things because of what she had said.

I was sitting in a deck chair next day, still thinking about the horse, when Mummy came out to find me.

'So this is where you are,' she said in tones of despair. 'What are you doing?'

'Nothing.'

'That's all you've done since we came here!' she exclaimed.

'Well, I'm going to do something now,' I said, getting up. 'I'm going to the village.'

It was a good thing she didn't ask me what I was going to do in the village, I thought, as I made my way to the graveyard. I searched through the long, overgrown grasses until I found what I was looking for – a tombstone to the beloved memory of James Baird, blacksmith, 1823–1865, murdered most foully in his own smithy by a brute horse, servant of the Devil. Mrs Thompson had not been making it up.

That night I sat up by the French window but, in spite of myself, I must have dozed off, for I awoke with a start to see the horse on the other side of the glass. I could see him plainly in the moonlight. His sides were rounded and glossy, his head proud, his neck arched with the noble stallion crest, but his eyes were desperate. It was a silent, tortured desperation I had seen in the eyes of worn out riding-school horses who were forced to go on working when all they wanted to do was rest. The horse needed my help. He wanted me to open the window and let him into the smithy. Just as I thought this, there was a crash of metal, making me turn, the screaming whinny, and when I looked out of the window again the horse was gone.

It was Wednesday night when I saw the horse again. I knew what I must do. I ran across to the French window, to where he was waiting. My hands were sweating and my legs felt like chewed elastic. I grasped the metal handle and pulled the door open.

Before my eyes the bedroom changed. Furniture and paint faded away. I crouched close to the wall, staring into the smoky depth of a smithy. The black-smith, a thin man with sandy hair, was working at the forge. Tied to a metal ring in the wall stood a black stallion. I was there to witness a scene that had taken place over a hundred years ago. I had opened the door, and now there was nothing I could do but watch.

'Come you up, then, my beauty,' called the smith in a cheerful voice, as he crossed the smithy to the horse, clapping its rounded shoulder. 'Stand you there, my man. Your master has deserted us, but if it's shoes you're wanting we'd best start now.'

The smith set to work, first trimming the stallion's feet, fitting the cold iron shoe, then casting the rough shoe into the heart of the forge to bring it out and hammer the glowing metal to the correct fit. As he did each foot, the smell of burning horn, as he pressed the glowing metal shoe against the hoof, filled my nostrils.

Three times the smith made a shoe, fitted it and nailed it on. There was only one of the hind feet waiting to be shod, and all the time the stallion stood without a movement. The smith stood over the forge heating the last shoe, and the horse turned and looked straight at me, as if he could see me out of the past, where I crouched, shivering and terrified.

The blacksmith came over to the horse, holding the glowing shoe on the end of a spike.

'Whoa, my beauty,' he murmured, as he approached the horse and laid his hand on its rump. 'Steady the man, we're almost through.'

At that moment the pincers that the smith used fell with a clang from where they had been leaning against the wall. At the noise, the smith turned round to see what had fallen. His foot caught on a bit of metal tubing that was lying on the smithy floor. He tripped, and the burning horseshoe fell against the horse's leg.

In a sudden panic of agony it lashed out and caught the smith on the head. The man crumpled and fell.

He seemed to roll limply into the hind leg of the horse, and it whinnied with a cry of fear. In a frenzy, the horse fought to free itself. The rope holding it to the wall broke, and, as people came hurrying to the smithy, the horse galloped past them and into the night.

The bedroom furniture became real again. The people crouching round the slumped shape of the smith faded like mist over the marsh. I was too tired to shut the French window, I staggered across the room, threw myself on the bed and slept.

When I awoke in the morning the French window was still open, and the dream, if it was a dream, the ghosts – if they were ghosts – came back to me. There was no Devil Horse, only an accident. The people themselves had dreamed up the Devil.

I told Peter, because I had to tell someone. He was annoyed because I hadn't told him sooner.

'I didn't want the parents to find out. They'd have fussed. But what are we going to do? I think the ghost horse is still there because people have gone on believing that he killed the smith. We must do something. No good trying to persuade Mrs Thompson that she's wrong, but there must be something we could do.'

'You mean to lay the ghost?' asked Peter. 'Settle its unquiet gallopings?'

'That's what he wanted me to do, I'm sure.'

'Sounds like that to me, too,' Peter agreed. 'I'll think.'

He did, and late on Friday evening, the last day of our holiday, we both set off for the village carrying a bag with a pot of Polyfilla in it and two knives for spreading it. We found the blacksmith's grave and very carefully filled in the words 'murdered most foully in his own smithy by a brute horse, servant of the Devil.'

'There,' I said when we had smoothed it off, 'that's it. People will forget now.'

'All the same, I wish you'd told me sooner. I've never seen a ghost.'

'He might not have been able to come if you'd been there,' I said. 'Perhaps he was waiting for someone like me. You'd see ghost birds if there were any around.'

We were to leave at dawn on Saturday morning, to give us time to drive home in one day. I was just climbing into the car when I remembered that I had left my book in the bedroom.

'For heaven's sake be quick,' said Daddy impatiently.

I dashed back to my bedroom, found my book under the bed and then, for a last, stolen moment, went to stare out over the marsh. Would the horse rest, now that I knew the truth? Now that the lies on the gravestone had gone forever?

Something glinting in the long grass of the garden caught my eye. I wrenched the French window open and ran to find out what it was. Lying on the grass was a horseshoe. It had not been there before. I picked it up. It was rough and heavy by today's standards. Holding it, I gazed over the marsh.

'It was an accident,' I said aloud. 'I know you didn't mean to kill the smith.'

A sudden wind blew a mad track through the rushes. Again I heard the stallion's whinny. It was no longer shrill with terror, but free and filled with ecstasy. The sound of our car horn drowned it.

I set the horseshoe on the bedroom mantelpiece where it belonged and ran to join my family, with the stallion's whinny of freedom echoing in my ears.

THE TOCKLEY FAMILIAR
by Kay Leith

North Throcton was a dead little place, especially at the beginning of October. If it had had any visitors that summer they were long since gone, leaving it to sink back into somnolence – if, indeed, it had ever wakened up.

The first week hadn't been too bad. Derek had met the son of a doctor and they'd done a bit of fishing, but since then there had been nobody around who was less than double his thirteen years.

His aunt, the only member of the family free to take Derek on a holiday, spent a lot of her time visiting local museums and churches and discussing her expeditions with another spinster with similar interests whom she'd met through the vicar.

For this Derek was grateful, for Aunt Greta was inclined to be a mite tedious about gravestones, brass rubbings and ancient parish records, and impatient with people who didn't share her mania.

As the second week began, Derek wondered if he might be driven, out of boredom, to doing just that! He'd exhausted the possibilities of the rocky coast, and there wasn't a street or alley in the neat and tidy North Throcton that he hadn't explored.

One day he walked beyond the small town, past the golf course and up the slight hill towards a wooded area. There wasn't much of interest except the fields and grazing farm animals, until about half a mile out, when he found a narrow road which didn't have any 'Private – Keep Out' notices.

The grass had grown through the surface in the middle of the road, which proved that it wasn't used much. He decided to investigate. If anyone asked him what he was doing there, he could honestly say that he didn't know he was trespassing.

There were pine trees on the right, over the wire fence, and a field on the left. Round the first bend he stopped, startled. In his path was a furtive-looking, middle-aged man who seemed even more surprised than Derek was himself.

'Excuse me,' said Derek. 'Am I trespassing, do you know?'

The man, who had a sack over his shoulder, said: 'Well, if you be, I be, too!'

'Does the road go anywhere?'

'As far as Tockley House, what's left of it, but I wouldn't advise you to go there.' The man put down his sack, lit a pipe and blew out clouds of pungent smoke. ''Tain't a good place.'

The boy was immediately intrigued. 'What do you mean?'

'Well, lad, 'tain't a place to go after dusk – or daylight neither! Nobody lives there no more, but things happen.'

'What kind of things? Has anything ever happened to you?'

'Off an' on,' said the man. 'Favourite silly game is throwing stones.'

'But, if nobody lives there, it must be somebody from the town playing a joke.'

'I'd like to catch 'im then, whoever he is. I'd give him stones, an' no mistake!' The man picked up his sack. 'You'd best come back along the road wi' me, lad.'

Derek shook his head. 'Thanks all the same, Mr . . . ?'

'John Biddle – general odd-job man and one-time thatcher.'

'I'm Derek Waverley, Mr Biddle. I think I'll go and have a look at the house, since I've come this far.'

'Well, it's up to you, Derek. But only look, mind. Don't go near the pesky place.'

'All right, Mr Biddle.'

The tumbled towers of Tockley House came into sight a quarter of a mile further on, standing on a slight hill. The gaunt rubble, in some parts, seemed like a disease disfiguring the pleasant scene, whereas in other sections smothering ivy made it appear almost as if the house were still whole and occupied. There were traces, as Derek noted as he edged closer, of what had once been formal and graceful gardens. Sweeping oaks and beeches stood in the spacious, unkempt parkland, and there was a long, curving weed-covered drive. A broken fountain stood in front of the house.

Derek stood looking up at the ruin. In spite of its bleak and baleful aspect, it was, after all, just an old tumbled-down house – the kind where one wouldn't be surprised if there were treasures buried somewhere within its walls. The people who had lived there must have been very rich.

John Biddle had said not to go near the place, but what did he mean by 'near' – ten yards, twenty yards, or what?

There wasn't any sound anywhere except the faint chirp of birds, and Derek started to walk slowly up the drive. He had just reached the fountain when a piece of brick came hurtling through the air and missed him by inches. He stopped, fighting the desire to turn and run.

What made him move forward again was the idea that someone somewhere in the ruins probably thought that it was funny to scare the daylights out of people. Like John Biddle, he'd give him 'stones' if he caught him – that is, if it wouldn't be more prudent to run! It all depended on his size!

The front door had long rotted and fallen in, and only one square column remained of the portico. Through the gap Derek could see the heaps of weed-shrouded rubble.

This time, as he was within ten feet of the gaping door, not one stone but several began to rain about him. Making a quick decision, and shielding his head, he ran for the ivied wall and crouched with his back to it. His heart was hammering like a steam press now, and uppermost in his mind was the problem of how he was going to get back down the drive again unscathed if the stone-throwing didn't stop.

'Come on out!' he shouted. 'Don't hide yourself like a coward!'

That let loose a fury of stones, as if all the spirits of the air were affronted by the accusation. They rattled all around him, striking his head and arms. Luckily the ones that hit him weren't very big – just enough to leave a small bruise. However, the odd thing was that they were coming from all directions, as though an army of urchins, spread around the grounds, were using him for target practice. But there was absolutely no sign of any living creature.

'Who are you?' Derek shouted.

As quickly as they'd begun, the stones suddenly stopped. The place grew as quiet as a mausoleum. The boy moved away from the wall slowly, ready to dive back to cover at the first hint of another fusillade.

Nerves jumping, he looked up at the gaping windows, and then, eyes searching, went through into what had been the entrance hall of the old place. There was no roof at all, not a single slate or joist in position, and Derek wondered if Tockley House had originally been burned down.

Suddenly there was a tremendous crash, and he spun round. Where he'd been standing only a moment before lay the remains of a coping stone. It was patently impossible for any human being to get up there, knock off the stone, and then hide – not unless he knew how to fly!

It occurred to Derek that it might have been pure coincidence – that the coping stone had required no help to push it free – but if he wanted to believe that he would be very naïve.

'All right,' he said aloud. 'I can take a hint. I'll go.'

The hairs on his neck prickled and his muscles twitched with strain as he determinedly and slowly stepped over the shattered coping stone and walked down the curving drive. He looked back before the house was lost to sight, but no jeering figure, or visible ghostly manifestation, watched his retreat. Yet, there was someone or something there at Tockley House – something very odd indeed . . .

Aunt Greta was in a mood at dinner. 'A little knowledge is a dangerous thing! Some people imagine, because they know a little, that they know it all! It's so tiresome!'

Derek surmized that she must have had a difference of opinion with someone. Her spinster friend, for instance?

'There's a big ruin not far from here,' said Derek temptingly. 'I shouldn't be surprised if it has some interesting lore connected with it. I'd ask at the Town Hall, only they're inclined not to take people my age seriously . . .'

'Hmmm. That's true,' said his aunt. 'Old, you say, and ruined? What's its name again? Hmmm. Yes. Well, I've got some time on my hands tomorrow. I'll find out what I can for you.'

Derek was drawn back to Tockley House next day, as though someone were pulling a string. He supposed it was the lure of the unexplainable, and until he'd found out what was going on, he didn't think he'd get much peace.

He stood about twenty yards away, looking and wondering. The place seemed to taunt him. He moved forward, and out of nowhere a jagged stone whizzed through the air and struck him above the eye.

Blood pouring down his face, he ran towards the house, hurt and furious. His handkerchief quickly became soaked.

'Come out, you coward!' he shouted to the uncaring walls. 'Coward! Coward! Coward!'

His voice reverberated defiantly. 'Coward! Coward! Come out! Beastly coward!'

There was a distinct tremor in the air, which the boy sensed, as though something were responding to his shouts.

'Beast!' He listened, walking forward slowly. 'Beastly coward! Beast!'

It was a mere whisper at first, like a faint rumble, but it grew and swelled and expanded until an angry gale was born. It howled in and out of the vacant windows, bent the ivy, flattened the mounds of weeds, roused the derelict dust into eye-stinging spitefulness.

Derek crouched on elbows and knees before the

165

portico, his hands and forearms shielding his head. The wind was filling his nostrils with grit, and it even got under his closed eyelids.

He lost track of time in the buffeting of the wind and the cuffs and slaps he received from unknown objects flung along by the force of the gale. Eventually it seemed to him that it was lessening, and he opened his eyes and looked. His blood froze with horror.

About four feet above the top step floated two coral-red slits! They stayed the same distance apart all the time and seemed like eyes. They bored right down into the boy's brain, and sweat broke out all over his body.

Derek knew then what it must feel like to be a rabbit mesmerised by a snake. He could not move! The eyes came nearer until they floated directly above him. He cringed, terrified.

Then, like a puff of smoke, they were gone!

For nearly ten minutes he remained crouched, utterly shattered, afraid to move. What was it he had seen? Certainly nothing human – nor animal either! A ghostly guardian, perhaps . . . The guardian of Tockley House?

But what was it guarding? Treasure? There seemed no other way to account for it.

Feeling dazed and shaken, Derek got to his feet. It was quiet and peaceful now, but at any moment the stones might start to fly, or the thing decide to return, so as quickly as his trembling legs would take him, he dashed directly across the weed-choked debris and down the drive.

He found his aunt in her favourite tea-room, having coffee with an old lady. Aunt Greta quizzed him about the sticking plaster on his forehead, but he'd already thought up a good excuse.

'This is Mrs Terence, Derek, and she's the owner of Tockley House.'

Derek looked at Mrs Terence with renewed interest and shook her hand. 'There's something odd about the house, isn't there, Mrs Terence?'

The old lady nodded, then described how her family had tried to re-build the house after the fire, but each time they'd had to abandon the project because the workmen wouldn't stay. It had acquired a bad reputation and even local farmers refused to graze farm animals on the land.

'As you can imagine,' said Mrs Terence. 'Not being able to sell it has meant great hardship for us. Grandfather Allan Broadfoot spent most of his money building the place, and when it was destroyed we were left almost destitute. From what I have been able to piece together from faint personal knowledge of him, and from what relatives have said, he was a peculiar man, and my grandmother left him several times and took the children with her.'

'However,' said the old lady, rising. 'Do come and have tea with me at Myrtle Cottage. It gets so lonely at times. I'd be so pleased . . .'

Had Derek told his aunt what he had seen she'd certainly have refused to let him out of her sight – if she didn't think he had become mentally deranged. That wouldn't solve anything, and it would only mean that his freedom might be curtailed, so he said nothing about the ghostly red eyes.

Later that day Derek met John Biddle.

'I say, Derek, don't say anything about that sack o' mine yesterday, will you?'

'No, of course not!'

'You see, a man has to feed his family as best he can . . .'

'I understand, Mr Biddle.'

167

'Call me John, lad. Now, tell me, what did you think of our ghostly mansion?'

Derek nodded. 'Ghostly is right! I saw something weird, John.'

Biddle's eyes gleamed with interest. 'What did you see?'

'Well, it's hard to describe. It looked like two red eyes floating about in the air. They were there for only a short time before they disappeared.'

'So . . . ! I always knew there was something!'

'Have you seen anything?' asked Derek eagerly.

'At times I've imagined there was a shape, but nothing substantial. 'Tany rate, it's better not to dwell on such things, Derek. There's a thoroughly nasty feelin' about the place. Wouldn't be no bad thing if somebody bulldozed it flat.'

'But the owner, Mrs Terence, says they could never get workmen to stay any length of time there.'

'Well, that's not our problem, me lad! We don't have to worry about that . . .'

'It seems a pity, though . . .'

'Well, I'd best be gettin' back to Station Road, or the wife'll put my dinner in the dustbin.'

The following afternoon Derek was made to comb his hair, wash his face and put on a suit for tea at Myrtle Cottage. It was a tiny place, crammed to the picture rails with Mrs Terence's collection of miniature paintings.

'I'd hate to have to sell any of these, but in last spring's gales some tiles became loosened, and something will have to be done about it.'

What space on the walls and on top of the furniture was not occupied by miniatures, was filled with photographs of the family.

'And that,' said Mrs Terence, indicating a full-length, yellowish studio portrait, 'is bad old Grandfather Broadfoot himself.'

Derek examined the protruding fierce eyes and the rat-trap mouth over the black beard.

'They do say that the awful man dabbled in things he oughtn't to,' Mrs Terence said, sensing Derek's interest. 'Rumour even had it that he had a familiar.'

'A familiar?' queried Derek, puzzled.

'Yes, a close companion. Usually it is an animal, a cat generally. People who have familiars are supposed to be able to change places with them, or be able to read their minds.'

'Was it a cat your grandfather had?'

'Nobody knew what it was, so the story goes.'

Aunt Greta gave a mock shudder. 'Good heavens! How ghoulish you two have become!'

'Well, you know how legends grow up about odd people,' said Mrs Terence, laughing. 'People just love making up stories about them.'

Derek wished the old lady would go on talking about her grandfather, but guessed that she didn't want to say more in case it would upset Aunt Greta.

However, an opportunity arose later when the latter was out of the room.

'What kind of things did your grandfather dabble in?' asked Derek.

'Well, nobody ever really found out, but he had a large collection of books on magic and the occult, and whatever he did, he did behind closed doors.'

She got up, opened a small cupboard and brought out a polished wooden casket. 'Grandfather Broadfoot's ashes!' she whispered. 'I don't know why I bother to keep them, except that I don't know quite what to do with them.'

'Bury them in the grounds of Tockley House,' suggested Derek. 'I'll do it for you, if you like.'

'What a good idea! Come and see me later and we'll talk about it.'

Aunt Greta's entrance halted any further discussion.

Well, it was all very well for Derek to be brave and say that he'd go to Tockley House, dig a hole, and deposit in it Grandfather Broadfoot's only remains. But what about the eyes? And the hail of stones? It's all very well being brave when you know what you are up against. Whatever it was that was haunting Tockley House was a very unknown quantity indeed.

Then he thought of John Biddle.

It wasn't too difficult to track down the house in Station Road. The door was opened by a short, plump woman with a cheerful face and slightly greying hair.

'Yes, of course, my dear. Come in. He's in the back garden . . .'

The thatcher was momentarily surprised to see Derek, but got on with his digging while the boy explained why he was there.

'That, my lad,' said John. 'Might be dangerous.'

'I know, John. That's why I can't do it alone and came to see you. Mr Broadfoot was a weird old man. The odd things that have gone on there might have something to do with him. Taking his ashes there, well . . .'

'Hmmm.' Biddle was silent for a long time. Then: 'Well, I'll try anything once, I suppose. Never ever dug a grave afore!'

'When, John?'

'Any time you like, lad, so long as it's not after dark.'

'Tomorrow morning?'

'Fair enough!'

Derek collected the casket from Mrs Terence and met the thatcher standing waiting at his front gate with a spade and two bicycles. 'We might want to get back down that road quicker'n we came.'

He'd also brought two pieces of wood which he said they could use as shields if the stones started to fly.

It was a pleasant sunny morning, but the sky seemed to darken when they came in sight of the house. Derek couldn't understand how he'd ever thought that it looked harmless.

'Where shall we bury the casket, John?' he asked.

'Well,' said Biddle, reaching to the heart of the matter. 'If we're supposed to be tryin' to exorcise this ghost or whatever, I think the hole should be dug as near to the house as possible.'

'All right.' Derek's mouth felt dry with fear as he started to push his bike forward.

They walked slowly and warily, watching the open spaces and blank windows for any sign of moment.

'I just hope that what we're goin' to do won't bring up the fiends of hell around us,' whispered John hoarsely.

Twenty yards, ten yards . . . They'd passed the fountain. When the first missile thudded to the ground they were startled, in spite of knowing that it would happen.

John unstrapped the pieces of wood, and they edged forward towards the front steps under the bombardment that rattled and thudded on the wood.

'Right here, in front of the steps.' gasped the thatcher. 'Can't get any nearer without goin' inside! Hold the wood over me while I dig the hole.'

Derek's unprotected knuckles and their legs took most of the onslaught.

'Won't be long now,' grunted John breathlessly. 'Reckon a couple of feet should be enough.'

Derek realized that the fusillade of stones was ceasing and looked around. His heart almost stopped. Crouching on top of the steps behind John Biddle was a thing. Derek couldn't shout a warning because his mouth and throat were too dry.

It was pale – a pale green – and its skin was pitted and deeply lined. The arms were short and thin and the hands clawlike. The long legs resembled a frog's. Its pointed ears twitched and two long fangs covered the lower lip. Its eyes were malevolent slits of coral.

The thatcher looked up when Derek's nerveless hands dropped their wooden shelters, and his eyes followed those of the boy's.

'Gawd!' whispered Biddle. 'What is it?'

The ears flattened as the man dropped the spade and its eyes blazed with fire.

How long they stood they could never afterwards hazard a guess. Derek had the horrible sensation that they might stand there for ever . . .

Slowly, slowly, John Biddle let his knees sag until he could reach the ground. The thing watched him, claws unsheathing.

'Careful, John!' begged Derek.

Keeping his eyes on the apparition, the man fumbled with the catch on the casket and flicked it open; then he pushed it towards the steps.

Finally, picking up the spade he pushed the casket closer still, until it was only a few feet from the steps.

The creature looked down. There was a sudden flare of red light from its eyes and, like a drift of smoke, something rose from the ashes inside the casket and took a vague shape. It appeared to be a tall figure – a man, a man with a beard – but later they could not be absolutely sure what they had seen.

Before the cloud of vapour enveloped the creature it emitted a squeal of delight and the ground seemed to shake with its purring.

Then, in a crack of lightning-like, blinding brilliance, the creature and the man disappeared.

When Derek and John examined the casket they found that it was empty.

'Let's put it in the hole, anyway,' said John.

'D'you think that it was waiting all these years for Allan Broadfoot to come back?' asked the boy, awed.

'Could be.'

'I wonder where they've gone . . .'

Biddle lit his pipe, sighed and wiped the sweat of fright from his forehead. 'Well, one thing's for sure – it won't be heaven, will it, lad?'

From that day the ruins and grounds of Tockley House were left undisturbed. Derek learned later that the farmer whose land abutted gave Mrs Terence a good price for it.

Only John and Derek knew about the reunion of Broadfoot and his familiar. As Biddle said: 'What's the point in talking about it? Nobody would believe us, anyway.'

ALICIA
Louise Francke

Sanderford is a yellow cat with yellow eyes and he is never allowed in the attic. But Elizabeth Ann had seen him go up, so she went after him.

She stopped five steps from the top of the stairs. The step that put her eyes just above attic-floor level. She stood quietly for a moment and looked along between boxes and bureau legs for a patch of yellow fur. 'Here Sandy, here Sandy,' she called softly.

The attic door had been standing open a little. That's strange, she thought. She had seen Sandy's tail disappearing into the darkness, so she knew he was here. 'Here Sandy, here Sandy.'

He wasn't allowed in the attic. Ever.

'Here Sandy, here Sandy.'

'Here, dear. He's over here, dear Alicia,' a sweet, soft voice answered. Elizabeth Ann froze. Her mouth dropped open slightly and her eyes grew wide with astonishment as they turned in the direction of the gentle but terrifyingly unexpected voice.

In the chair. In the dainty great-great-grandmother rocker. A pale pretty, white-haired woman in a delicate blue dress. Right next to the chair sat Sanderford with his tail curled neatly around him. Both of them were looking at her.

'Here, dear.' The woman's hand drifted down slowly to touch the top of Sanderford's head. 'Here's your kitty. With me. You see? Your kitty is my friend, dear Alicia.' She was smiling. But her eyes

174

didn't smile. They seemed hard and brilliant in the dim light.

'My name is not Alicia,' said Elizabeth Ann in a faintly choked voice.

'I know. I know, my dear.' She spoke softly but quickly. 'But you do look like Alicia. You look so very much like Alicia I really don't believe I can call you anything else. You won't mind if I call you Alicia, will you? I have thought of you as Alicia for so long. Ever since I started watching you play in the garden. Right from this window.' She motioned towards the small window and her hand looked nearly transparent. 'I was hoping you would come. Today. Especially today. Because today you are eleven.' Again she smiled sweetly.

Today was, in fact, Elizabeth Ann's eleventh birthday.

'But don't just stand there on the stairway, dear Alicia. Come up, come up.' Her voice was soft but urgent. 'I've been waiting so long to talk with you.'

Elizabeth Ann didn't want to go up. She thought she should go down and tell her mother about this woman sitting in the attic.

'Come,' insisted the woman. 'Let me show you the picture of my beautiful Alicia. You'll see. You'll see how much you look like her.'

'No thank you. Not right now.' Elizabeth Ann knew that this woman should *not* be sitting in the great-great-grandmother chair in the attic. 'I must go now.' Then she remembered why she had come to the attic. 'Here Sandy, here Sandy,' she called, but Sanderford's tail remained curled around his paws. 'Here Sandy, come Sandy.' The pale woman had reached into a blue pocket and was holding a small picture out towards her.

'Come and see Alicia first, my dear, and then I

will let your Sanderford go with you.' What did she mean, *let* him go, wondered Elizabeth Ann. Did she have the power to make him stay there?

No, Elizabeth Ann didn't want to go up. But she put her foot on the fourth step from the top, slowly. Perhaps she would just look at the picture quickly, then take Sandy downstairs. Her foot moved to the third step.

'Yes, yes, come dear. Here it is.'

Elizabeth Ann had reached the top and was walking cautiously towards the woman in the chair. Then, with a wave, the picture came fluttering through the air.

As she bent to pick it up from the floor, Sanderford uncurled his tail, walked across the attic and down the stairs.

Elizabeth Ann followed. On the fifth step from the top she turned her head to look at the woman once more, but the great-great-grandmother chair was empty. Quite empty.

Elizabeth Ann shut the attic door firmly.

Silly, she thought. Silly! Silly imagination. Yes, it is. Yet she had the picture in her hand.

She looked at the pale, reddish-brown portrait. At the small face looking back at her. It's *me*, she thought. It really does look like *me*.

She turned the picture over and read the pencilled inscription: 'Alicia Frost, Aged 11.' Then she walked into her room and slipped the picture, face down, into her dressing-table drawer.

Elizabeth Ann waited until after dinner. Until she and her mother were alone. She had made her wish, blown out the eleven birthday candles . . . and they had had ice-cream, too.

Now she was drying dishes as her mother washed.

'Who was Alicia, Mother?'

Her mother was slipping more plates into the dish-water and hardly seemed to notice the question. 'I don't know, dear. Who was she?'

'I don't know either,' answered Elizabeth Ann. 'But she was somebody. I found her picture in the attic. On the back it says she's Alicia Frost, aged eleven. That's my age now. And she looks just like me.'

'Alicia Frost?' Her mother thought a minute. 'Attic? Well, there are some old things in the trunk up there, I think, but I don't remember any pictures. Frost,' she repeated. 'That was your great-grand-mother's name. Yes . . . yes . . .' She frowned thoughtfully. 'Alicia Frost was your great-grand-mother's sister. She died when she was a little girl.'

Elizabeth Ann picked up another plate and rubbed it with the linen towel.

'But . . .' her mother continued, 'I don't remem-ber ever seeing a picture of her. Where did you find it? In the trunk?'

'I picked it up off the floor.' There, thought Eliza-beth Ann. That's the absolute truth. There's no imagination about that.

'Where's the picture now, dear?'

'In my room.'

When the dishes were finished, Elizabeth Ann brought the picture down to show her mother. She was almost sorry that she had mentioned it, because now she wanted to tell her mother about the woman in the chair. Yet she knew it would sound foolish. Of course there was no woman in the attic. Even Elizabeth Ann knew that. She had simply imagined it. Hadn't she?

'Yes,' said her mother. 'That would be your great-grandmother's sister. She must have died right after this picture was taken. It was said that *her* mother – and that would be your great-*great*-grandmother, Elizabeth Ann – went quite mad after her little girl died. And that she wandered around the house for years, searching and calling for her daughter Alicia.'

'And that's her chair – my great-great-grandmother's chair – in the attic, isn't it, Mother?'

'Yes, that's right. Just think, it has been in the family all these years.'

'Do you think I look like Alicia?'

'Well, I think you do.' Elizabeth Ann's mother had put on her glasses and was studying the faded picture.

She handed the picture back to Elizabeth Ann. 'Yes, I think you look a lot like Alicia.' Then she patted her daughter's hair softly and said, half to herself, 'both very pretty girls, very pretty indeed.'

The matter was thus dismissed, and Elizabeth Ann didn't really think much about it again until the next afternoon when she was on her way to her room. She heard a faint call. 'Alicia-a.' She heard it. Distinctly. Definitely. She turned and saw the attic door standing open again.

Elizabeth Ann's heart pounded. I didn't hear it, she commanded herself. I'm imagining it. I won't go. I won't go up again.

'Alicia-a.' Faint and soft, but clear.

I won't go. She's not there. She doesn't exist. I'm imagining her. And Elizabeth Ann marched over, shut the attic door, turned her back and went to her room to change her clothes.

She never thought that she might have to pay for her rudeness.

Elizabeth Ann wakened from her sound sleep that night to see Sanderford glowering at her from the foot of the bed, his eyes too bright in the darkness.

And behind him stood the woman from the attic, but this time she was not smiling and her eyes were hard and brilliant.

'I called you,' she whispered with a tight mouth. 'You didn't come. You are a wicked girl. We had been waiting all afternoon and you didn't come.'

Her tone frightened Elizabeth Ann and she drew the eiderdown closer to her chin. 'You belong in the attic . . .'

But the woman interrupted, hissing at her, 'When I call you, you come . . .'

Tears of fright welled up in Elizabeth Ann's eyes, her mouth opened to call her mother, but nothing came out.

Abruptly, the expression on the woman's face changed and became both sweet and sad. Sadly sweet.

'Oh my dear, dearest Alicia . . . I didn't mean to frighten you. I missed you, that's all.' She was moving, noiselessly, up from the foot of the bed. 'Now that we've finally met, you're my own dear Alicia, and I want to see you often. Every single day.'

'Go back to the attic,' Elizabeth Ann sobbed softly. 'Go back to the attic . . .'

'Of course I will, my dear, dear girl. Of course I will, right now.' Her pale hand fluttered up towards Elizabeth Ann's cheek and she touched it softly with what seemed to be real affection. 'Just promise, my dear heart, you'll come and see me tomorrow. Come and talk to this lonely old lady.'

'I promise,' – though Elizabeth Ann hardly knew she had said it.

Without a sound, the woman drifted quickly towards the door and was gone. Sanderford closed his eyes, curled his paws under him on the bed and was asleep.

The morning was bright when Elizabeth Ann woke with only a vague remnant of an unpleasant dream in the back of her head. She looked at the bottom of the bed where Sanderford was stretching himself awake. He blinked at her and she blinked back, slid out of bed, went to the bathroom and washed her face, looking up into the mirror as she dried it on the soft towel.

There on her right cheek was a small strawberry-red mark about the size of a pea. Elizabeth Ann leaned toward the mirror and rubbed it. The skin was smooth and unbroken. Now what's that, she wondered. And her left-over dream flashed into focus. She stared at the red mark. That's where the woman had touched her. It's a warning. It must be. No! There is no woman . . . no woman at all. She must have dreamed that the woman had touched her the instant some mosquito had pierced her cheek. That's it, she convinced herself. But she rubbed it in doubt on the way down to breakfast.

Mother examined the red mark carefully and agreed with her mosquito theory. 'I'll spray your room this morning, so you won't be bitten again tonight.'

Elizabeth Ann was preoccupied with her dream all day. As bedtime approached, she became more and more uneasy. Perhaps she should tell her mother. But she knew what the reaction would be – a teasing laugh and a comforting pat with all of the blame given to her lively imagination. No, there was no point in telling anyone.

Bedtime arrived and, for the first time in her life, Elizabeth Ann looked under the bed and into her wardrobe before shutting the bedroom door. And, for the first time in her life, she locked the door, turning the key quietly . . . very quietly. Locking bedroom doors was forbidden. What if someone felt ill in the night and called out?

She propped herself up comfortably with her pillow and turned out the light. I'll just stay awake tonight, she told herself. And she did. For almost an hour.

Then it happened.

Elizabeth Ann was jolted awake by a hard, hurting jerk on her left leg. So hard, it pulled her right off her pillow and her head thumped back on the bed.

Instinctively, she twisted slightly to pull her leg towards her and there, at the end of the bed, was the woman, smiling sweetly, ever so sweetly, with her eyes burning bright in the dark. Both of the woman's hands held Elizabeth Ann's ankle tightly.

Sanderford stood, arched, on the bed, puffed and huge, nearly double his normal size. His mouth was open in a near grin, his eyes furious and glowing.

She heard the hissing whispers . . . 'It's time now Alicia-a . . . time to come. You broke your promise to me . . . you promised me . . . you promised to come . . . but you broke your promise . . . you made me come to get you . . . so I'll take you . . . with me . . . now . . .'

Elizabeth Ann struggled, but she was being pulled slowly towards the foot of the bed.

'I'll teach you . . . you'll come with me . . . you can't break your promise to me . . .'

Elizabeth Ann tried to scream, and tried again, but her breath was coming in short gasps as she fought to free her ankle.

'We'll go together now . . . the three of us . . .

forever together my dearest, my dearling . . . my own . . . Alicia-a.'

Elizabeth Ann pushed, but slipped on the smooth sheet. There was nothing for her hands to grasp. The eiderdown bunched and puffed and turned into soft nothingness in her fingers. She pulled and twisted and hunched her shoulders, but slowly, slowly she was being drawn towards the old woman.

Suddenly, Elizabeth Ann pulled herself upright and grabbed at the hands holding her ankle. She pried at the fingers of one bony hand and felt them weaken, slowly . . . slip . . . let go . . . *her hair*! The woman had seized her hair! One strong hand still held her ankle fast, but the other now gripped her hair and was pulling her head . . . ouch . . . ouch . . . ow-w-w-w . . . In her pain, Elizabeth Ann clenched both hands into fists and punched out into the middle of the not-so-fragile old woman. She heard a loud *hi-s-s-s-s* of breath as the woman doubled up. The hands let go.

Quickly, Elizabeth Ann rolled off the bed and, as her feet touched the floor, Sanderford's puffed, furry, yellow mass hurled itself towards her, claws digging into her shoulder. Her mouth dropped open and, this time, a piercing scream came out . . . a scream of pain as the cat's claws slid off her shoulder and down her back.

A hand clamped on to her wrist as Sanderford hit the floor with a thud. Elizabeth Ann whirled to face the woman and to pry, again, at the fingers holding her. In the distance there was a pounding on the door, and her mother's voice called, 'What's the matter, Elizabeth Ann? What's the matter? Why have you locked the door? . . . Elizabeth Ann?'

Her arm was being twisted and she was being pulled now, towards the window. The pounding turned to heavy thuds as Elizabeth Ann shrieked again. The woman's voice was still hissing in her ears, louder now, more cracking. 'You'll come . . . I have you . . . you're mine now, Alicia-a . . . you're mine . . .'

An agonizing twist of her arm and Elizabeth Ann fell against the window. So hard, the latch gave way and the window swung open. She felt herself being pulled out . . . out . . . out into the night. She grabbed the side of the window frame with her free hand, grabbing hard . . . for her life.

The bedroom door crashed open, the lights flashed on and, instantly, all was quiet except for Elizabeth Ann's choked sob as she slid to the floor by the window.

She heard her mother cry out and felt her father pick her up and carry her downstairs.

She couldn't answer the questions as they cleaned the blood from the claw marks on her shoulder and back, but she shook her head and mumbled, 'No . . . no . . . it's not his fault . . .' As horrified accusations were hurled at Sanderford, wherever he was hiding.

Then Elizabeth Ann took a deep, trembling breath and said, 'The chair. The great-great-grandmother chair in the attic . . . Burn the chair . . .' and the whole strange story came tumbling out.

By the time the story was finished, Elizabeth Ann's shoulder and back were softly wrapped in a clean, white bandage. They were all gathered in the kitchen and it was beginning to get light outside.

Elizabeth Ann stopped talking. She was exhausted. Her mother and father had listened and now sat with her in silence. After a few long minutes, her father rose. He went upstairs to the attic and brought down the dainty, dusty rocking-chair.

He carried it across the kitchen and out through

the back door to the garden, where he put it down. Then he brought old newspapers out of the garage and, one by one, crumpled the sheets and tucked them under the chair.

Mother and daughter stood together, holding hands as they watched through the doorway. Elizabeth Ann's father struck a match and lit the papers in several places. The tiny flames licked around the seat of the great-great-grandmother rocker. It was very old, very dry, and the flames leaped on to it, consuming it quickly as the three of them stood, transfixed, watching the smoke curl into the morning sky.

Elizabeth Ann felt a soft tickle on her leg and looked down. Sanderford was with them, watching too, rubbing himself gently against Elizabeth Ann's leg and rumbling loudly with loving purrs.

THE TERRIBLE GAOLER
by Rosemary Timperley

Hot. Hot and white. A little white building at the edge of the Moroccan village. Deserted, too. Nothing around it seemed to move, except the four people approaching it: Roger, his father and mother, and the guide, Ahmed.

'What is it?' Roger asked.

'Nothing,' said Ahmed, 'but once it was a prison, in the bad old colonial days when the French were our masters. Now we have good, up-to-date Moroccan prisons.' He said it proudly, as if they were luxury hotels.

Roger liked the way Ahmed spoke of the 'bad old days'. At home, grown-ups nattered on about the 'good old days', making him feel as if he'd missed out on something.

'Can we go inside?' he asked.

'If you wish. It is only a ruin now. Not locked up. Anyone can go in, and come out again. Best sort of prison, no?'

'Depends on your point of view,' said Roger's mother. 'I don't want to go inside. I'd rather sit under that tree and steam gently. My feet are like burning coals.'

'Mine too,' said his father, looking from his own shoe-encased feet to Ahmed's sandalled ones, with impertinently curling toes. 'You go and look in the prison, if you like, Roger. Your mother and I will sit here in the shade and Ahmed can fill in the gaps in our history.'

Roger was off like a shot. Much as he liked Ahmed, he found the guide's potted history lessons a bit much. It was all very well for his parents to enjoy them. They didn't have to have history lessons at school.

'So, I tell you the history of the prison,' Ahmed was beginning, like any old schoolteacher, as Roger, with a delicious sense of adventure, made his way alone towards the little white building. The sun burned down on his head. A bit dizzy-making. It was a relief to enter the shadowed doorway of the ruin.

Parts of it really were ruined, with bits of the roof missing, but there were a few scruffy little cells still intact. He looked around hopefully for old bloodstains or mysterious Arabic carvings on the walls; for instruments of torture or even an ancient ball-and-chain. But there was nothing like that. The place, he thought, was a bit like an outside loo without the actual loos. Frankly, it was boring. And so hot. He felt slightly sick with the heat. Indeed, he nearly went straight back to his parents and the guide under the tree, but pride made him stay a little longer.

He sat down on the floor in one of the cells. He'd thought he was quite alone in the place. Then suddenly he saw a large man standing there. He hadn't seen or heard him actually enter. It was unnerving. He got to his feet and backed away a little.

The man was wearing a grey jellabah – that dressing-gown thing that many Arabs wear – and a grey turban was wrapped around his head. Yet he didn't look like an Arab.

'What are you doing here?' he asked Roger. He had a rough voice and a strong cockney accent.

'Only looking round. The guide said I might.'

'Where do you come from?'

'London.'

'You and me both.'

'Are you on holiday, too?' Roger asked politely.

'Nope. Business. I'm looking for my head.'

'Your what?' Roger thought he must have mis-heard.

'Head. Head. The thing that should be on my shoulders.'

'But it is,' said Roger.

'Nah!' The man shook the head he said he hadn't got.

Oh, lor, thought Roger, a nutter. This was a word of which his father, a doctor who specialized in psychiatry, did not approve. All the same, this chap must be a nutter. A nutter who thought he hadn't got a nut. Still, it would be pretty awful to go through life thinking you hadn't got a head, so Roger decided he must be kind. 'How do you think you came to lose your head, then?' he asked nicely.

'Lose it? I didn't exactly lose it. It was took. They chopped it off, that's what,' said the man.

'Who did?'

'The prisoners. They called me 'The Terrible Gaoler'. They called me a lot of other things too, which I won't besmirch your ears with.'

'Besmirch?'

'Dirty. Soil. Make mucky. Bad language makes little boys' ears turn black and drop off, if they hear too much of it.' He laughed.

'You mean you were a gaoler here in the bad old colonial days?' Roger asked.

''S right. It was my last job. Before that I was a mercenary soldier. That's one who fights for any old side as long as he gets paid. I was with the French occupation force. Then I got a wound which made me unfit to fight, so they gave me this job. I did it so well, though I says it as shouldn't, that they began to send all the worst criminals here. The sort of thieves and murderers who'd stop at nothing. Real, rip-roaring villains. But I was a match for them. I controlled them, all on me tod.'

'How?'

'By being villainous back. Chains to keep them still. Beatings to keep them quiet. If they didn't behave, they got no food. They soon behaved. When inspectors came, they were amazed at the nice, quiet little community I founded. None of them ever escaped while I was here. "Over my dead body," I used to say. And that was how they all did escape, in the end.'

'Over your dead body?' said Roger.

''S right, mate.'

'But you're *not* dead.'

'I am, you know. Dead as a door-nail. Only I'm earth-bound, see? On account of not being able to find my head. And it's a damned sight worse than being egg-bound, which is saying something.'

'It must be terrible,' said Roger, humouring the man. He added delicately: 'I think perhaps you're what my father would call "disturbed".'

'Your father would be dead right. I'm very disturbed indeed. So would you be if you'd had your head chopped off.'

'What exactly happened when they did the chopping?'

'Prison revolt, that's what happened. They must have been plotting it for weeks, the villains. They put some dope in my food – I'll never know how they got hold of it; I wouldn't let them smoke their hashish in here, but I expect that's what it was. I passed out. My "trusty" – Huh! I was a fool to trust him – wasn't chained. Well, I had to have someone to wait on me, didn't I? He took my keys, unlocked the rest, and by the time I came to I was trussed up like a chicken and they were preparing a bonfire, like on Guy Fawkes night, with me as the intended guy.'

'Or like Joan of Arc,' suggested Roger.

'Not at all like Joan of Arc. She was a holy lady, I was a wicked man.'

'Yet you'd been put in charge of criminals, like a good man.'

'Good men are no good with criminals. They don't understand them. I did. I didn't blame them for having revenge on me. I'd have done the same in their shoes. Not that they wore any. No, when they'd got me all ready for burning, I said: "Look, I've only been doing my job. You're on top now and you're going to do me in. Fair enough. But a man about to die should be able to choose how. I don't fancy burning. Too painful. Nor hanging. Too undignified. But beheading – that's what they did to Marie Antoinette and Charles the First. So you be good lads and behead me. You can burn me after, if you like, as I shan't feel nothing then". That was my request. I didn't understand about death then, you see. I thought it was the end. If I'd known it was going to be like this, neither in one place nor the other – '

'But you're not dead,' Roger burst out. 'It's all in your mind.'

'I don't know what's in my mind! It's in my head and I haven't got my head! Of course I'm dead. All this happened a hundred years ago or more. I've lost count. Do I look like someone a hundred years old?'

'Well – sixty, maybe – '

'Sixty! Are you being funny? Thirty-five. Huh!

That shows you're only pretending that I've got a head. If you could really see it, you'd see the young face.'

'I'm sorry,' said Roger. 'Everyone over sixteen looks much the same to me – thirty, forty, sixty. But I'll tell you how we can prove that I can really see your head. Take off your turban and I'll tell you what colour your hair is.'

'Waste of time. You're a fibber, or you're mad. You see, they did behead me, as I asked, and after they'd done it, they untied the rest of me and just left me lying there. They started dancing around the fire, like a lot of dervishes, and I got up and walked away – the way a chicken goes on trotting about with its head off. It was only when I was miles away that I realized I'd forgotten to pick up my head and take it with me. I've been haunting this place ever since. I've looked everywhere. It's not fair, you know. Anne got hers back.'

'Who's Anne?'

'Anne Boleyn. Henry the Eighth's bird. She doesn't wear it, just carries it under her arm.'

'And walks the Bloody Tower,' agreed Roger.

'None of that swearing! Keep a clean tongue in your head. I'd have had you in chains for that in the good old days.'

'Please,' said Roger, 'let me convince you that you have got your head all right. Let me take your turban off and see your hair. Don't tell me what colour it is. *I'll* tell *you*.'

He stretched forward, and the man didn't resist. He felt the turban with his fingers. He wondered what material it was made of, so soft and light it was, like fine ash or cobwebs, with a whiskery, whispery feel against his fingers. He unwound the strange material and revealed the man's hair.

He received quite a shock. He'd expected it to be dark. It wasn't. It was red. Brilliant red. Bedazzling.

'You have *red* hair,' he said quietly. 'Very, very red. No one could *imagine* such hair. *Now* do you believe that you've got a head?'

'Well, blow me down,' said the other. 'Do you mean I've been looking for my head all these years and it's been on my shoulders all the time?'

Roger nodded happily, feeling, he imagined, rather as his father must feel when he'd finally cured a patient of some miserable delusion.

'You've got a head with lots of red hair on it, *and* you're not dead. You can believe that too now, can't you? I think myself that you're not the Terrible Gaoler at all. You're a person who's been reading bits of history and sitting in the sun too long, and it's all got sort of mixed up. Come and meet my parents. My father's a doctor. He'll help you far more than I can – although I've made a start. Fancy you thinking you were beheaded and deaded! You almost had me believing you sometimes!'

'It's a rum do,' admitted the man.

'Come and meet my father. Follow me.'

Roger went ahead. The man began to follow. Roger walked away from the prison, then looked behind and saw that his 'patient' was not following any more. He was returning to the prison, his great big back view with its flame of red hair somehow pathetic and beaten, as if he *had* to stay where he was, even when he didn't want to.

Roger was about to call, then stopped. For he had noticed something strange. Something so very strange that his heart raced with fear, and he turned and ran across to his parents at top speed. Suddenly he didn't understand anything any more.

'Hello, darling,' his mother greeted him lightly. 'Are you running away from the Terrible Gaoler?'

He stared at her.

She went on: 'You should have stayed for Ahmed's history lesson. It was just your bucket of blood. Ahmed has been telling us about the "bad old days", when the Terrible Gaoler controlled that prison. He was an Englishman, a giant with red hair, who terrorized the prisoners until they rose up against him, went berserk, beheaded him, and were going to burn him – but his body mysteriously vanished without trace, all but the head.'

'The body did not vanish,' Ahmed said darkly. 'It walked away. It is walking still. It haunts the prison, seeking the lost head. But the Terrible Gaoler will never find his head because they burned it on their bonfire until there was nothing left but the finest ash.'

Roger stood perfectly still, the heat of the sun reaching down to him like flames of an inverted bonfire. He remembered the fine-ash feeling of that grey turban . . .

'Darling, what's the matter?' His mother's voice, fading into distance. He blacked out.

He came to in his hotel bedroom, his father hovering around.

'What happened?' he whispered.

'A touch of the sun. My fault. I should have watched and warned. Some doctor I am!'

'It wasn't only the sun,' said Roger, remembering now. 'It was the Terrible Gaoler. I met him in the prison. I thought he was a man who was mentally sick. I was bringing him to you, but he wouldn't come. He couldn't, of course. He's bound to that place, looking for his head. Yet I did get him to believe that his head was there, on his shoulders. It

192

must have been a spirit head, still the same, even after it had been burned to ashes. He was a sort of half-and-half person, neither quite dead nor quite alive. Earthbound, he called it, worse than being egg-bound – '

'Quietly now, old boy. Drink this and go back to sleep,' said his father, not believing a word of his story.

His mother had come in. 'What was Roger saying about being egg-bound? We haven't eaten any eggs lately.'

'He's a bit delirious, poor old lad,' said his father.

'He was ever so strict,' Roger went on dreamily. 'When I mentioned the Bloody Tower, he said he'd have had me in chains for using that word, in the "good old days". Ahmed's "bad old days" were his "good old days".'

'Who's he talking about?' his mother asked his father.

'He thinks he met someone in the prison. He didn't, of course.'

Having swallowed his medicine, Roger began to drift off to sleep. He had a swift, dreamlike image of the Terrible Gaoler, tiny and complete, pictured on the dark background of the lining of his eyelids. And the image turned into a proper dream, in which the Terrible Gaoler said: 'I couldn't come and meet your parents, lad. They'd have seen through me. I feel ever so much better, since seeing you. It *is* all in the mind. I'll never be quite normal, so I'll stay in the little white prison. It's home. And now I know I've got my head on my shoulders, I can relax. I'm sorry I frightened you when you left. I shouldn't have let you see me in the sun.'

Roger remembered this dream when he awoke. He didn't really understand it, except for the apology at the end. For what had frightened him so terribly when he saw his 'patient' returning to the prison was the shadow which the half-and-half-world man had cast on the white wall.

It had been the shadow of a man without a head.

THE GHOST TRAIN
by Sydney J. Bounds

Billy Trent ran down the lane towards the common, sandy hair poking like straws from under his school cap, eyes gleaming with excitement. The common blazed with coloured lights, post-box red and dandelion yellow and neon blue. The evening air throbbed with the sound of fairground music and his pulse beat in rhythm.

He reached the entrance and passed beneath a banner that read:

Biggest Travelling Fair in Britain!

A jolly, red-faced man dressed as a clown called to him. 'On your own, son? Enjoy all the fun of the fair.'

Billy nodded eagerly, too excited to speak, for the fair came only once a year and he'd saved hard for the occasion. Almost a pound's worth of change clutched tight in his pocket, he darted between the coconut shy and a hamburger stand, chair-o-planes and swing-boats. He paused, fascinated, in front of the merry-go-round with its pairs of magnificent horses going round and round and up and down. He stared up in awe at the big Ferris Wheel revolving in the sky, trying to make up his mind which to try first.

There were dodgem cars, and a snaky switchback ride. Music played, fireworks exploded in cascading showers of light. The smell of candy floss tempted him. For Billy it was the best night of the year, until –

In a shadowy empty space behind the fortune teller's tent, he found himself between two youths dressed in jeans and leather jackets studded with stars.

The big one with the scarred face gripped Billy's arm. 'Hi, kid, we'll give you a break – you can pal up with us tonight. It's more fun sharing things. I'm Ed, and my mate here answers to Higgy.'

Higgy, fat and pimply, sniggered in a way that gave Billy gooseflesh. 'Hi, pal, glad to meet yuh. Ed and me's broke, and that ain't much fun, so I hope you've got plenty of cash. We're all pals together, see?'

Billy shook his head, mute. He had a sinking feeling in his stomach and his hand tightened round the coins in his pocket as he stared up at the two older boys. He decided he didn't like either of them.

Ed's big hand tightened on his arm till it throbbed with pain. 'Now come on, share the loot – reckon we'll all go on the dodgems first, okay?'

Billy gasped desperately. 'You're hurting me. All right, I'll pay for you to have one ride, if you promise to leave me alone after that.'

Big Ed laughed meanly. 'That's no way for a pal to talk. Share everything, that's our motto, ain't it, Higgy?'

'You bet. Now then, kid, hand it over.'

As Billy slowly brought his hand from his pocket, Ed relaxed a fraction, grinning at Higgy. Instantly Billy twisted like an eel, slipped from Ed's grasp and ran off as hard as he could go.

'Little perisher,' Ed shouted angrily. 'Just wait till I get my hands on 'im – I'll break 'is flaming neck!' With Higgy at his heels, he gave chase.

Billy pushed his way into the fairground crowd,

panting, looking for someone – anyone – he knew. But they were all strangers, intent on enjoying themselves and oblivious to his trouble. The music blared loudly and bright coloured lights flashed.

Billy glanced back; the two youths were still after him, and Ed's scarred face looked savage. He ran behind a wooden hoarding and found himself trapped between the Wall of Death and the switchback ride. It was dark and he could see no way out. The roar of motor-cycle engines was deafening; even if he shouted, no one would hear. He hunted for somewhere to hide as Ed and Higgy turned the corner and spotted him.

Dim blue lights spelled out:

GHOST TRAIN

Billy could just make out the shape of a miniature steam engine with six open carriages in the gloom. The carriages were empty. There seemed to be no one about, not even at the pay desk.

As the train began to move towards the dark mouth of the entrance tunnel, Billy ran forward and sprang into the carriage nearest the engine. He crouched low, but –

'There he is!' Ed shouted, pointing. Higgy right behind him, he put on a spurt and they reached the train in time to scramble aboard the last carriage.

The Ghost Train gathered speed as it rumbled into the tunnel. In the darkness, Billy gulped as he looked up to see the luminous skeleton-figure of the engine driver grinning back at him. But he was too scared of his pursuers to be really frightened.

Then Ed and Higgy started to climb over the empty carriages towards him.

The track wound and the carriages swayed and rattled. Cobwebs brushed Billy's face. An eerie green glow illuminated the tunnel and a tombstone beside the track; the stone lifted and a cowled figure rose with a dreadful wail.

It was night-black again and a woman's scream echoed. In a phosphorescent glow, a headless phantom stalked towards the engine, vanished. Chains clanked and something evil-smelling dripped from the roof. A bat-thing swooped, hissing.

The dark came again. Then a lightning flash revealed a fanged monster.

The train rattled on through the blackness. A red glow from a fire showed three witches stooped over a cauldron: as the train passed, the nearest lifted her death's-head and cackled with laughter.

Suddenly Billy was aware that the two bullies were no longer interested in him. The skeleton-driver of the Ghost Train had left his engine and was moving steadily back along the carriages towards them. Ed's face had lost its savage look. Higgy's eyes no longer gleamed with malice.

As a bony arm extended, skeletal finger pointing, they backed away. Empty eye-sockets stared sightlessly at them, jaws gaped in a toothless snarl. A hollow voice intoned: 'Beware!' And, scared stiff, Ed and Higgy scrambled back to the last carriage.

The ride ended and Billy got away smartly. As he mingled with the crowd, he saw Ed and Higgy – their faces white as chalk – hurrying towards the exit. They'd had enough.

Billy looked again for the Ghost Train, but he could not find it now.

Left alone, he enjoyed all the fun of the fair. He went on one ride after another until he'd spent his money. He was very happy as he turned to go home.

On his way out, the clown called to him again. 'What did you like best, son?'

Billy Trent paused and thought. 'The Ghost Train,' he said.

The clown's jolly red face paled. 'But there's no Ghost Train now! Used to be one, with Old Tom driving, dressed all in black with a skeleton painted on. Then one day a youngster fell off the train and Tom dived after him. Killed he was, saving the lad. After the accident, the boss scrapped it – so you must have dreamed that.'

But Billy was quite sure he hadn't.

PORTRAIT OF RHODA
by Lucy Norris

'Oh, Sarah, it's beautiful!' chorused Lorna and Irene Edwards, gazing with wide-eyed admiration at the roomy four-poster bed with its dainty silken drapes. 'Are we really going to sleep in it tonight?'

Lorna and Irene were identical twins and often spoke in unison. Sarah Parker smiled fondly at them. 'But of course you are,' she confirmed. 'When I invite my best friends home for Christmas I try to grant their every wish. You said you wanted to sleep in a four-poster; and so you shall.'

'Good old Sarah,' said Lorna, giving her a pat on the back. 'We really are grateful to you. When Mummy fell ill we faced the prospect of a dreary Christmas with Aunt Edna. Instead, here we are living in the lap of luxury.' She swept her hand around the room. 'I know you told us you lived in a family mansion, but we didn't expect anything as fantastic as this.'

'It is a lovely old house, isn't it?' said Sarah with justifiable pride. 'It was built by my great-great-grandfather, Mortimer Parker; and Parkers have lived here ever since. My father was born in that bed.'

'How romantic,' sighed the twins.

Sarah glanced at her wrist watch. 'Good, it's tea-time. I'm starving. Come on you two, I smell crumpets cooking. Lovely, lovely crumpets with oodles of butter and honey.'

'You're supposed to be on a diet,' Lorna reminded her as Sarah led the way down to the lounge. 'You boasted to Avril Sinclair you would lose half a stone in weight before next term.'

'I know I did,' admitted Sarah, 'but I wasn't feeling hungry at the time.' She sighed enviously. 'You two don't know how lucky you are to be slim.'

'We wouldn't be if we ate as much as you do,' said Irene bluntly, but not unkindly. 'I'll be your conscience for the next three weeks, Sarah. Every time you start to over-eat I will stop you. Agreed?'

Sarah looked down at her plump figure and then at Irene's slim one. 'Agreed,' she said with misgivings, as she led them into the lounge where her mother was waiting to serve them tea in front of a roaring log fire.

Mrs Parker welcomed them and began to hand round dainty china plates. 'I'm sure you girls are hungry after your journey here.' She smiled at the twins. 'Lorna dear, help yourself to a crumpet, or would you prefer buttered toast?'

Sarah gave a little giggle. 'That's Irene, Mummy.'

Mrs Parker looked from one twin to the other and shook her head. 'You are so alike. I don't think I shall ever be able to tell you apart.'

'It's quite simple really, Mummy,' laughed Sarah. 'Irene parts her hair on the right; Lorna's is parted on the left. L for Lorna and L for left. And to make it even easier for you, Irene will be the ones who keeps frowning and tut-tutting each time I reach for a second helping of anything.

Irene certainly kept an eagle eye on Sarah. By the time they went to bed that night Sarah was convinced she had already lost weight.

Lorna awoke some hours later to find a bright beam

of light shining straight into her eyes, dazzling her. Before she could call out, a hand pressed down over her mouth and a voice whispered:

'It's all right, Lorna. It's only me.'

The hand was removed from her mouth and Lorna hissed angrily: 'Really, Sarah, if this is your idea of a joke . . .'

'No, honestly, I wasn't trying to frighten you,' whispered Sarah. The light from the small torch she carried threw strange shadows on to her face, giving her a peculiar, grotesque expression.

'What were you doing, then?'

Sarah raised a warning finger to her lips. 'Please don't wake Irene,' she pleaded. 'She wouldn't understand.'

'Understand what?'

'That I won't get a wink of sleep tonight unless I have something to eat.'

'But it's the middle of the night,' complained Lorna. 'Everyone's in bed asleep.'

'I know that,' nodded Sarah. 'That's why I want you to come down to the kitchen with me. I'm too scared to go alone. Be a sport, Lorna. I'd do the same for you.'

Lorna was about to refuse when she remembered that if it hadn't been for Sarah's kindness, she and her sister would be spending a miserable Christmas with Aunt Edna.

'Oh, all right,' she agreed, slipping silently out of bed to avoid waking Irene. Pulling on her dressing-gown, she tip-toed after a jubilant Sarah.

They made their way by the light of the torch but, once downstairs, Sarah switched on the hall light, and together the girls ran along to the kitchen. It wasn't until Lorna stepped on to the cold kitchen floor that she realized she had forgotten to put on her slippers.

'Do hurry up,' she pleaded as Sarah rummaged through a large cupboard, opening a variety of tins. 'My feet are frozen. What are you looking for, anyway?'

'That chocolate fudge cake Irene wouldn't let me have at teatime,' replied Sarah, licking her lips in anticipation.

Lorna hopped from one foot to the other. 'A plain biscuit would be less fattening,' she said reprovingly. 'I dread to think what Irene will say when you tell her you've been guzzling a cake in the middle of the night.'

'I have no intention of telling her,' replied Sarah. She wrenched the lid from yet another tin. 'Aha! Success at last! Like a piece?'

'No, I wouldn't. And please hurry. I'm cold.'

Sarah found a knife and helped herself to a slice of the cake. 'Sure you won't have some?' she enquired before putting the tin away.

'Quite sure,' Lorna said firmly. Her eyes widened as she caught sight of the generous slice Sarah was holding. 'If you eat that you'll not only get fatter but you'll come out in spots as well,' she warned.

'You're probably right,' agreed Sarah comfortably, 'but it will be worth it.' She took a large bite and sighed blissfully.

Lorna regarded Sarah's bulging cheeks with disgust. 'May we go back to bed now?' she asked hopefully.

'When I've eaten this,' Sarah said with some difficulty, speaking out of the side of her mouth. 'If you're feeling cold, we can sit in Dad's study. He always has a fire half-way up the chimney so I'm sure it won't have burnt out yet.'

It hadn't. In fact, the firelight was so bright they didn't bother to put the room light on, but curled up on the thick furry rug and, while Sarah contentedly ate her cake, Lorna warmed her icy toes.

'If only I didn't like sweet things it would be so easy to diet,' sighed Sarah between mouthfuls. 'You won't tell Irene about this little indiscretion, will you?'

Lorna didn't answer. She was gazing intently at a lifesize portrait of a young and very beautiful lady holding a red rose in her hand. The portrait was on the wall opposite the fireplace and in the flickering light the painting looked most life-like.

'Isn't she beautiful!' exclaimed Lorna. 'Who is she?'

'Her name was Rhoda, which is Greek for rose,' replied Sarah. 'During her lifetime she kept vases of roses in her room all summer long and always wore a rose-scented perfume.'

'Was she a relation of yours?'

'Wish she had been,' sighed Sarah, 'then I might have inherited some of her beauty. On the other hand, knowing my luck, I would probably have inherited her vile temper instead.'

'Did she have a vile temper?' Lorna studied the sweetly-smiling face. 'I find that hard to believe.'

'So did my grandfather, Henry Parker,' sniffed Sarah. 'He met Rhoda Marston when she was eighteen. They met at a hunt ball and he fell head over heels in love with her. At first he refused to believe the stories he was told about her temper but it wasn't long before he found out for himself.

'Henry had arranged to go riding with Rhoda but had to cancel this when his mother asked him to act as host in his father's absence. Henry explained his problem to Rhoda but she insisted he should keep his date with her.'

'What happened?' asked Lorna.

'What didn't happen!' Sarah rolled her eyes dramatically. 'That evening when Henry and his mother were seated with their guests at dinner, they heard a horse galloping. It was Rhoda, riding at breakneck speed across the lawn. When she reached the terrace she halted the sweating beast and shouted for Henry. The french windows to the dining room were open – it being a hot night – and she could see Henry sitting at the table.

'Henry's youngest sister, Clare, was present at the dinner party and she wrote a full account of the affair in her dairy; that's how we know all about it,' said Sarah, fortifying herself with the last mouthful of cake. 'When Rhoda shouted for him, Henry turned very white but continued to entertain his guests. Rhoda grew more and more angry and – you'll never believe this – she actually rode her horse up the terrace steps and in through the open french doors. Imagine it! She actually rode into the dining room! Rhoda's horse, Magic, reared and pranced before the astonished diners while Rhoda, her long hair cascading wildly around her shoulders, struck at Henry with her riding whip.'

'Poor Henry,' exclaimed Lorna.

Sarah nodded. 'Clare wrote that he behaved magnificently. In spite of the danger from the horse's hooves, to say nothing of the whip, he caught hold of Magic's bridle and tried to soothe the frightened creature.

'Rhoda was furious. She screamed at Henry to leave her horse alone, and struck at him again. The horse reared and bumped against the table, knocking several wine glasses to the floor. The glasses were part of a family heirloom. Rhoda knew this and laughed with pleasure. She cried: "I'll teach you to break a date with me!" then leant forward and swept several more from the table with her whip.'

Sarah lowered her voice to a stage whisper.

'And then the most awful thing happened . . .'

'What?' gulped Lorna.

'Rhoda's horse, frightened by the smashing glass, reared suddenly. Rhoda lost her balance and was thrown to the ground, and . . . the most terrible thing . . . one of the horse's hooves struck her face, cutting deeply across her left cheek.

'Rhoda went hysterical. She grabbed a knife from the table and attempted to slash at Henry, but by now the horrified guests had gathered their wits sufficiently to come to his aid. Rhoda was carried screaming from the room and taken home. She was kept under sedation for weeks.'

'What about her face?' asked Lorna as Sarah paused to lick the last crumbs from her fingers. 'Was she badly scarred?'

'Hideously so,' said Sarah with almost ghoulish delight. 'She refused to go out or allow anyone to visit her. Apart from her family, the only person to see her after the accident was the artist who painted that portrait.'

'Was that painted after the accident?' asked Lorna.

'Yes. That's why she has turned her head so that you can't see the left side of her face. Rhoda heard about a wandering artist – some say he was a gipsy but, whatever he was, he claimed he could paint a person's soul into their portrait. Rhoda had him paint that portrait of her and when, a year later, Henry married Isobelle Richmond, Rhoda sent him that painting as a wedding present.

'There's poor taste for you! Poor old Henry married to a plain-looking but sweet-tempered girl and Rhoda sends him that gorgeous portrait of herself.

They say Isobelle was very upset, so Henry put the painting in here – and here it has remained ever since.'

'What happened to Rhoda?'

'Oh, yes. I nearly forgot to tell you the best bit! After sending Henry that painting, Rhoda killed herself! She plunged a dagger into her heart and with her dying breath she cursed poor Henry and vowed he too should meet a violent death.

'And he did! A year to the day after Rhoda died, Henry was found murdered: in this very room!'

Lorna gave a gasp of horror and began to shake all over. Sarah regarded her with amusement.

'You've never struck me as the nervous type,' she observed dryly.

'I'm not,' Lorna shivered. 'I don't know what's the matter with me, honestly I don't. I have the most terrible feeling that something awful is going to happen. Tell me, Sarah. Who murdered Henry?'

Sarah shrugged. 'They never found out. Poor Henry was slumped in that chair, a stab wound in his chest. His eyes were wide open and the expression on his face was one of – well, horror, they say. Clare wrote in her diary that she believed *she* knew who had murdered Henry but that no one would believe her.'

'Who did she think it was?' asked Lorna, rising to her feet, her face as white as chalk.

'She didn't say,' shrugged Sarah. 'I think we ought to go back to bed now, don't you?'

Lorna stared up at the portrait. 'She did it!' she said positively. 'She killed Henry.'

Sarah looked at Lorna in surprise. 'You're talking nonsense. Rhoda had been dead a year when it happened. How could she have done it.'

Lorna's face was very pale, her body shaking all

over. She spoke in small sobs. 'Show us how you did it, Rhoda,' she gasped. 'Show us, I dare you!'

To Sarah's horror the painted head moved, turned and stared down at them. A look of intense hatred shone in the vivid blue eyes; a hatred directed at Lorna. The figure rose and stepped from the frame. Sarah heard the rustle of the stiff silk dress; saw the hideous scar. An overpowering, almost suffocating scent came from the red rose in Rhoda's hand.

Terrified, the two girls clung to each other, mesmerised with fear and unable to protect themselves.

From the folds of the silken gown the slim white hand withdrew a small dagger. Menacingly, she advanced towards them, the hand raised ready to strike.

In the shadows of the doorway behind her a scream rang out. Rhoda swung round and gave a startled cry when she saw Irene standing there. Irene, pale and shaking, continued to scream again and again.

Rhoda stared from one twin to the other. The sight of identical girls standing either side of the room seemed to bewilder her and she backed away.

Sarah, jerked into action by the screams, pulled Lorna across the room. Lights were switched on all over the house as disturbed sleepers rose from their beds to investigate the noise. Grabbing the twins, Sarah ran from the study and along the hallway. At the foot of the stairs they collided with Sarah's father.

Trembling, sobbing, they told him what had happened.

'Something woke me up,' cried Irene. 'I found Lorna was not in bed and I knew, I just knew she was in danger somewhere, so I came to look for her.'

'And if Irene hadn't screamed when she did, Rhoda would have killed us,' cried Sarah. 'As it was, I nearly died of fright when Rhoda stepped from that picture frame.'

'This I must see for myself,' said Mr Parker. He strode towards his study, followed, at a safe distance, by the three nervous girls.

Switching on the light he walked in. The girls peered cautiously in from the doorway. The portrait was as it had always been. Rhoda Marston gazed gently down, a smile on her lips, a look of innocence in her painted eye.

'But I don't understand . . .' exclaimed Sarah.

Mr Parker smiled gently. 'When you told Rhoda's story to Lorna, it started her imagination working. Somehow, Lorna made you believe it was possible for a painting to come to life, and then you both let your imagination run riot.'

'But what about Irene?' persisted Sarah. 'She didn't know about Rhoda, yet she saw her.'

'Telepathy,' said Mr Parker in that matter-of-fact way of grown-ups. 'It's a well-known fact that people – especially twins – can transmit thoughts to each other, even when many miles apart. Lorna imagined the portrait was alive and put the idea into Irene's mind. Now girls, back to bed. In the morning Sarah, I would like an explanation as to why you and Lorna were downstairs at all.'

'So would I,' hissed Irene as they trundled upstairs. 'What were you two doing, anyway?'

'Don't tell her, Lorna,' said Sarah, brightening considerably as an idea occurred to her. 'Let her guess!' She beamed upon Irene. 'Lorna will send you the answer by telepathy! Imagine the fun we can have!'

'No, thanks,' exclaimed Irene. 'I've had quite enough imagining for one night.'

'I suppose we did imagine it all,' said Lorna. 'I

mean, a painting couldn't really come to life . . .
Could it?'

'I guess not,' sighed Sarah. 'Pity. It would have
made a smashing story to tell the girls at school.'

Downstairs in the study a red rose petal lay un-
noticed on the floor beneath the portrait. A rose petal
as garden fresh as the day it had been picked.

And red roses don't grow in December.

THE RED MILLER
by Mary Danby

Paul Barratt lay in bed, listening to the whispers, trying to make some sense out of them. 'Hush!' they seemed to be saying. 'Hush!' Only he wasn't making any noise. He waited. In a little while, the groaning would start, and the silky, soothing voice that said: 'Shoo-sha . . . shoo-sha . . .'

Shivering, Paul clutched the bedclothes around him and stared out into the darkness of the little round room. It was empty except for his bed, a small chest of drawers, a bookshelf and the huge, wooden pillar that came up through the floor and disappeared into the ceiling. Sometimes, he thought he could hear a moaning noise and frantic scratchings coming from inside the pillar, as if there were people trapped inside. He imagined them being skeleton-thin, dressed in rags, growing feebler as the years went by, their moans becoming weaker and weaker . . .

'You've enough stories in your head to fill a book,' his mother would say. But there was more to it than that. The noises Paul heard at night were real – so real that they kept him awake, sometimes for hours, and he would screw himself up into a sobbing, trembling ball under his blankets and pray that they would go away.

In the rooms below, his parents and brother Angus slept peacefully, unaware of the night-time terrors that gripped the youngest member of the family. When he was little, Paul had often run to his parents'

211

room. 'There's a witch behind my wardrobe!' 'There's a snake under my bed!' Now that he was ten, such behaviour seemed babyish. Anyway, he would have had to go through Angus's bedroom to reach his parents, and he was anxious not to let his brother see his tears.

He had always been sensitive – 'highly strung' his mother called it – even before they had come to live in the windmill. But here, in this strangely-shaped, out-of-date building, sticking up awkwardly on the edge of a busy, modern town, he had heard and seen things which he was sure were more than just products of his imagination.

He had lived in Garston all his life, and used to pass the windmill on his way to school. About three hundred years old, it had been used for grinding corn until around 1900. It was a tower mill – a tall, brick-built, conical building – with rooms on five floors and a wooden balcony running all the way round it, and, unlike many old mills, it still had its sails. They no longer turned, though, and many of the shutters were missing or hanging loose.

For a long time after the last miller had died, the old mill had been left empty, then a market gardener had bought it and removed all the internal machinery so that he could use it to store his produce. In the 1950s it had become the home of an artist, and now it was the turn of the Barratts. Paul's father, the manager of a local butcher's shop, had long had his eye on the place, and when it came on the market he was quick to put their box-like semi-detached up for sale and make a good offer for Garston Mill. 'Be quite a talking point, won't it, Joyce?' he had said to Paul's mother. 'How many of our friends can say they live in a windmill, eh? And fun for you boys, too,' he had told Angus and Paul, 'living somewhere with a bit of character. Perhaps we'll get the sails working again one day. Be a bit of a project, that.' Angus had been very excited, but Paul knew, as soon as he stepped inside the mill, that he wasn't going to like it. The atmosphere was strange and stuffy, and he found it hard to breathe. 'There's something unhappy in here,' he told Angus.

'Oh really, you are soggy,' said Angus, and his mother said: 'Leave him alone, dear, he's highly-strung.'

In a way, living in the mill was like being in a very tall, narrow house, except that all the walls were curved, so that none of the furniture fitted properly. On the ground floor, there was a small entrance hall and cloakroom, and a spacious living-room. From the hall, stairs went up to the kitchen, which had a small sitting-room leading off it. Paul and Angus used this as their 'den' – they considered themselves too old to have a playroom. On the next floor were their parents' bedroom and a bathroom, above that was Angus's room and, right at the top, the sail-room, where Paul slept. In the days when the mill was working, it had housed sack hoists and gear wheels, driven round by the sails. All that now remained was a section of the windshaft, which jutted out high up the wall. Paul's father had fitted a false ceiling below it, to keep out the draughts.

The great wooden pillar in the centre had once carried the power from the turning sails down to the millstones in what was now the living-room. Where it passed through Paul's room, he had stuck a poster of some seagulls on to it. Angus copied the idea, only his section of the pillar sported posters of pop groups and football stars.

The two rooms were connected by a stout wooden ladder that came up through a hole in Paul's bedroom floor. Getting the bed up there had been quite a problem – they had had to take it to pieces first – and it now stretched right across the tiny room, so that Paul had to climb over it to reach the small, round window.

On some days, he would stand for ages at his window, like Rapunzel trapped in her tower. A long way beneath him was the overgrown back garden of the 'Red Miller' public house, and, beyond it, a supermarket car park. But he could see a great deal further than that. He could see right across Garston to where the marshes disappeared into the grey sea-haze. Once, there was probably a view of cornfields, but the nearest thing to agriculture now was a row of allotments next to the supermarket. It would not be long before they, too, would be built on, Paul supposed.

The first few weeks of living in the mill were full of fascination and a feeling of strangeness. Paul and Angus helped their parents to repaint the rooms and arrange the furniture, to hang curtains and to sort out the neglected garden. Then, as the excitement died down, Paul began to notice another feeling. It began when he was alone one afternoon in the den, reading a book. he found himself listening and, in the uneasy silence, turning to look over his shoulder, as if he had heard someone come into the room behind him. Later that night, as he stood looking out of his bedroom window at the lights of Garston scattered beneath him, he thought he heard someone sigh. When he looked round, there was nobody, but he could see traces of a kind of light mist hanging in the air.

From then on, bedtime held nothing but terror for Paul. He would make one excuse after another not to go upstairs. When at last he went to bed, he would lie awake listening for the noises – for the sly, whispering voices and tormented groaning. Then a continuous, rhythmic creaking would begin, and grow and grow until it filled his little room and seemed to turn his head over and over, over and over. When, finally, he could see and hear nothing more, he would fall into a restless sleep.

One morning at breakfast, Angus said: 'Honestly, Paul, I get no peace with you up there. You thump about all night. Keeps me awake.' He bit crossly into a piece of toast.

'Is that right, Paul?' asked his father. 'Aren't you sleeping well? Pass the butter, will you, Angus?'

'You do look a bit peaky,' said Mrs Barratt, putting a hand under Paul's chin and turning his head towards her so that she could study him.

'It's noisy up there,' Paul began tentatively. 'I can't get to sleep.'

'Noisy?' said Angus with his mouth full. 'All I can hear is you crashing about all night.'

'Yes, yes, all right,' his father told him. 'What noises, Paul?'

Paul shrugged. 'You wouldn't understand.' He almost added: 'You're a butcher.' After all, butchers spent their days hacking carcases to pieces. How could they understand something as subtle as an unseen presence?

'Yes, we would, wouldn't we, Eric?' said Paul's mother. 'Well, go on, then, tell us. You'll have to be quick, mind,' she went on, 'because your father's got to be at the shop by eight-fifteen.' She placed a cigarette between her coral-pink lips, lit it slowly and blew smoke across the breakfast table. 'Well?' she said, making a listening face.

Paul knew he was doomed before he began. He

215

looked hopelessly down at his plate. 'This mill . . . it's full of secrets,' he said quietly. 'Full of sadness.'

'These sad secrets – what *sort* of secrets, dear?' asked his mother, looking bemused. 'Do try and be more specific.'

'I hear things,' Paul said.

His father nodded. 'Yes, yes, we know that. But what do you hear?'

'Voices, whispers.'

'What do they say?'

Paul bit his lip. 'I don't know.'

Angus stood up and took his plate over to the sink. 'If you ask me,' he said, 'he's loony. I should have him put away.'

'You're a big help, you are,' said Joyce Barratt, flicking ash into the saucer. 'Tell you what, Paul can sleep in your room tonight. See if that helps. All right, dear?'

And that was the end of the conversation. Mrs Barratt began the washing-up, Mr Barratt went off to work, and the two boys got themselves ready for school. Paul felt utterly trapped. Persecuted as he was by the terror surrounding him, he was unable to be rid of it, because nobody else would understand.

On their way to school, they passed the small public house that Paul could see from his bedroom window. They had seen 'The Red Miller' many times before, but it had never occurred to Paul to wonder who the name referred to. The inn sign bore a painting of their mill, standing alone amid fields of wheat sheaves. 'Who was he, do you think?' Paul asked Angus. 'The Red Miller, I mean.'

'Some Communist, I expect,' said Angus. 'They're always called "Red Somebody-or-other".'

That night, Mr Barratt put up a camp bed for Paul in Angus's room. Angus grumbled, because it left little space to move about in. 'You are soppy, Paul,' he said. 'And if you've brought your noises with you, I'll sock you one.'

Their mother, overhearing him as she came upstairs to say goodnight, said: 'I won't have you being nasty to Paul. If *you* had a bit more more of an imagination, you might get better marks in English.'

'Mum,' said Paul, 'do you know who the Red Miller was?'

Mrs Barratt sat on the end of Angus's bed. 'The one the pub was named after? I think he was the last miller here. Died around the turn of the century, I believe – at least, that's when the mill was last in use.'

'Why was he called Red? Was he a Communist?'

'I don't think so, dear. They didn't have them in those days.'

When the lights were out, and their mother had gone downstairs, Angus pulled a comic from beneath his pillow and switched on a torch. He read for a while, then looked over to where Paul lay silent and wide-eyed on his camp bed.

'You're thinking about that miller, aren't you?' he said softly.

Paul nodded.

'Well, actually, he was a mur-r-r-der-r-r-er-r-r,' said Angus, in a creepy kind of voice. 'He was red with the blood of little children who strayed into his mill. He ground their bones into the flour, and that was the end of them.' Angus held the torch under his chin, so that it lit up his face with a ghostly glow. 'The mad red miller of Garston Mill,' he intoned. 'You can still see the gore dripping down the walls.'

'Oh, shut up!' said Paul in a high voice. He could feel the tension building up. His chest felt tight and

217

his skin pricked with fear. Long after Angus had switched out the torch and fallen asleep, he lay awake . In a little while, he heard a far-off creaking, rattling sound, which came nearer and nearer. It was saying something, but he couldn't quite make it out. Yes – yes, he could, now. It was saying, quite clearly: 'Mur-der-er. Mur-der-er. Mur-der-er.'

The next day was a Saturday. In the afternoon, Mr Barratt asked Paul to help him to scrape the paint off the door that led from the entrance hall to the living-room. At present, it was a gloomy dark brown, and they decided to give it a coat of fresh white gloss. First of all, though, the peeling paint had to be removed.

Paul's father held a blow-lamp to it, and the two of them were busy scraping when Paul suddenly sat back on his heels and put a hand to his throat.

'What's up?' asked his father. 'Got a sore throat?'

'No,' Paul said wheezily. 'I can't breathe properly. The air feels – kind of thick.'

'We'll take a break,' said Mr Barratt. 'Here – come and sit down for a minute.' He opened the front door, and the two of them sat down side by side on the step.

'Better?' asked Mr Barratt, as Paul took a few deep breaths.

'Yes, I think so.'

'Funny, isn't it,' said Mr Barratt, gazing round at their small garden, 'How this place is getting to you. If it's not noises, it's feelings, vague worries, some-thing in the air. I think you must be psychic.'

'What's that?' asked Paul.

'Oh, you know – one of those people who can tune into things that the rest of us ordinary mortals are unaware of, thank the Lord.' He scratched the back of his head. 'So, what are we going to do about it, eh? You can't really expect us to move house every time you get a funny feeling.'

Paul flushed. He felt hot and embarrassed.

'It isn't just "funny feelings",' he said sulkily. 'I think there's something peculiar here – something real. I think . . . I think it's haunted,' he said abruptly.

His father gave him a sideways look. 'And who – or what – is haunting it? A mad miller, perhaps?'

Paul turned swiftly. 'Yes! How did you know?'

Mr Barratt laughed, and patted his shoulder. 'I didn't. I was just joking. You don't think I believe in ghosts, do you?'

Paul subsided again. 'No, I suppose not,' he said dejectedly. 'But there *is* a ghost, you know. The Red Miller. And Angus says he was a murderer who killed little children and ground their bones into the flour.'

'Really?' said Mr Barratt, raising his eyebrows. 'And how would Angus come by all that information?'

'I – I don't know,' said Paul. 'But afterwards, I heard this voice, and it said "Murderer". Honestly, Dad, I'm not making it up.'

Paul's father got to his feet. 'I know you *think* it's real,' he said, 'but it seems to me your imagination has been running riot. Murderous millers, ghosts in the woodwork.' He chuckled. 'Next thing, you'll be seeing blood dripping down the stairs, like in all those dreadful horror films.'

Paul was silent.

'Tell you what, old chap,' his father went on. 'You do me a favour and go along to the ironmonger's for a bottle of white spirit, will you? I'll just finish get-

219

ting the old paint off, then we can start on the under-coat.'

When Paul returned with the white spirit it was beginning to grow dark. Long clouds hung in stripes across a dirty pink sky. Anxious and depressed, not knowing whether he should be feeling angry or afraid, Paul walked with his head down, watching his feet take him along the pavement. Then, as he turned into the driveway leading up to the mill, he heard a rumbling noise, and looked up. He couldn't believe what he saw.

Above him, the sails were slowly turning. Stark and black against the setting sun, they went round and round, shifting their position slightly every now and then to catch the breeze.

Paul was astonished. His father couldn't possibly have fixed them in the short time he'd been out. Anyway, he was busy working on the door – wasn't he? Paul could hear sounds from the mill, only not of blow-lamp or paint scraper. Lights were on, too – every room seemed to be aglow – but it was a soft, shining light, more gentle than he was used to. Tentatively, he approached the front door.

Inside the mill, there was no cheerful hall or living-room. It was all a big space, with an enormous cog-wheel revolving above his head. On either side, great grindstones turned, devouring the grain which fell in golden streams from the hoppers above. 'Shoo-sha . . . shoo-sha . . .' went the grain. 'Hush!' as another load of grain fell from the bins to the hop-pers. All around, the air was cloudy with flour. Paul, white-faced and shaking, stumbled around, trying to understand what he was seeing. There was no warmth here. It was cold – cold as death, he thought, trembling.

'Dad?' he called nervously. 'Dad?'

He began to climb the ladder to the floor above, though he knew there would be no kitchen there, no den or television. There were sacks. Row upon row of them. And he could feel beneath his feet the grain that had spilt on the floor. The noise was constant. Above him, the sails creaked round and the cog-wheels groaned and grumbled. The great wooden pillar throbbed with life, and the sack hoists carried their loads from floor to floor. Paul recognized all the sounds as his eerie companions of the night.

He heard footsteps, then saw a pair of boots, white with flour, descending the ladder towards him. The miller. Rigid with terror, Paul waited. It was as if all the fear, all the terrible uncertainty, had been the prologue to a nightmare. And now it was time for the nightmare.

In a moment, the miller would be at the foot of the ladder. Then he would turn, and Paul would see . . . what? The face of a murderer? Hands wet with the innocent blood of children? And would he be the next victim?

The giant cog-wheel rumbled round and round. 'Mur-der-er,' it said in a rattly voice. 'Mur-der-er.'

And the miller turned.

One glance at his terrifying face sent Paul falling backwards on to one of the sacks with a cry of fear. The miller came towards him with outstretched hands.

But these were no murderer's hands – they were upturned, pleading – and the face was not grim at all, Paul realized, once he had recovered from the shock. Indeed, the miller had a rather pleasant, jolly face, chubby and smiling. The only thing that marred it was the huge birthmark that covered all but one side of his forehead. A strawberry mark – red as blood.

'Of course,' thought Paul. 'The Red Miller.'

The Miller spoke. His voice echoed, as if it came from a great distance.

'Please . . .' he said beseechingly. 'Don't be afraid of me. I never hurt anyone.'

Paul stared, and the miller went on: 'Don't run away . . . don't be afraid . . . please . . . please . . .'

The voice was slowly fading, and the miller, too, seemed to be slipping away. A cold mist swirled through the mill and Paul could see nothing else for a few seconds. Then the mist cleared, and he was no longer leaning on grain sacks; he was in the den, propped against the soft arm of a chair.

He blinked several times and felt slightly sick, as if he had just stepped off a roundabout. Then he heard his father calling from downstairs.

'Paul? What are you doing up there? Did you get the white spirit? Come and help me finish this door.'

Paul made his way unsteadily out of the den, wondering whether he should say anything. If he told his father he'd seen a ghost, he would only be laughed at.

'I got what you wanted, Dad,' he said as he reached the ground floor, 'and – '

His father waited for him to continue.

'And while I was out, I – well, you see, I sort of made up my mind about something,' Paul said in a rush. 'I don't want to be . . . psychic, or whatever you said. You know, all that highly-strung stuff. I don't want to be different, if you see what I mean. I think I won't make a fuss about this place any more. O.K.?'

He stopped out of breath, and watched his father's expression change from surprise to delight.

'Well done, old son!' said Mr Barratt. 'So you're going to be a man after all, not some snivelling mouse.'

Paul flinched.

'All these noises you've been hearing. All in your head, of course. But I knew you'd grow up one day. I said to your mother, 'Give him time,' and I was right, eh?'

Nonsense, thought Paul. He knew it had nothing at all to do with growing up, and, as he lay in bed in his own room that night, waiting for the comfortable creak of the sails and the swishing of grain in the bins, he whispered: 'I'm not afraid of you, miller, really I'm not. I won't run away.' But though his ears probed the silence for whispers and his eyes peered through the darkness for a glimpse of that poor, disfigured face, the mill was silent and peaceful.

After a while, Paul turned over and went to sleep.